Po
#4

The COLOR *of a* DREAM

By
Julianne MacLean

NEW MADRID COUNTY LIBRARY
309 E. MAIN ST.
PORTAGEVILLE, MO 63873

Copyright © 2014 Julianne MacLean
This book is licensed for your personal enjoyment only.
All rights reserved, including the right to reproduce this book, or a portion thereof, in any form. This book may not be resold or uploaded for distribution to others.

This is a work of fiction. Any references to historical events, real people, or real locales are used fictitiously. Other names, characters, places and incidents are the product of the author's imagination, and any resemblance to actual events, locales or persons, living or dead, is entirely coincidental.

ISBN: 1927675103
ISBN 13: 9781927675106

Prologue

Jesse Vincent Fraser

Sometimes it's difficult to believe that coincidences are simply that: *coincidences.*

How could it be that easy when the most unlikely events occur and we find ourselves connecting with others in ways that can only be described as magical?

Until recently, I didn't believe in that sort of thing—that fate, destiny, or magic played any part in the outcome of a man's life. I always believed that what happened to me later, when I became a husband and father, resulted from the decisions and choices I made along the way, with a little luck—good or bad—tossed into the pot for good measure.

Things are different for me now. How can I not believe in something more, when what happened to me still feels like a dream?

It's not difficult to pinpoint the exact moment when my world began to shift and all the puzzle pieces began to slide into place. It was a month before Christmas almost twenty years ago. A heavy, wet snow had just begun to fall.

I was fourteen years old, and it was the day I began to hate my older brother.

Chapter One

Some people said we lived in the middle of nowhere because the road wasn't paved and ours was the only house for many miles.

I didn't think it was nowhere. I liked where we lived on the distant outskirts of a quaint little town where our father was the only dentist.

I suppose it was a bit remote. Once you drove past our house, which stood at the top of a grassy hill with pine trees behind it, you reached a bend in the road and were suddenly surrounded by thick forest on either side. It was extremely dark at night.

That didn't stop people from speeding, however, because it was the only alternate route between our town and the next and there were plenty of country folk who preferred to avoid the interstate. Partly because our road provided a more direct route into town, but mainly because it was where the bootleggers lived. If you wanted liquor after hours—or if you were underage—a fifteen-mile drive down a deserted gravel road was only a minor inconvenience.

More than a few times, we were awakened in the night by drunks who drove into the ditch where the road took a sharp turn not far from our home. We always left our outdoor lights on all night, so we were the first house they staggered to. Luckily, the ones who came to our door were always polite and happy drunks. There hadn't been any fatalities and my father never refused to let them use the phone to call a tow truck.

The event that changed my relationship with my brother, however, occurred in the bright cold light of day during the month of November, and we weren't coming from the bootlegger's shack. We were on our way home from a high school football game where we'd just slaughtered the rival team—thanks to my brother Rick, who was captain and star quarterback.

Earlier in the day, Rick had been coerced by our mother to let me tag along to the game. Now he was dropping me off at home so that he and his buddies could go celebrate.

As we turned left onto the gravel road, the tires skidded and dust rose up in a thick cloud behind us. Rick was doing the driving and I was sandwiched into the back seat between two keyed up linebackers.

"Did you see the look on the other coach's face when you scored that first touchdown?" one of them said. "We were only five minutes into the game. I think that's when he knew it was going to get ugly."

"Ugly for them, but not for us," Greg said from the front seat. He high-fived Rick, who lay on the horn five or six times.

The car fishtailed on the loose gravel as he picked up speed, eager to get rid of me no doubt.

"Hey," Greg said, turning to speak over his shoulder to Jeff, the linebacker to my right. "What are you going to do if Penny's there?"

I may have been only fourteen years old, but I'd heard all the gossip surrounding the senior players on the team. They were like celebrities in our town and if the school could have published a tabloid, these guys would have been on the front cover every week.

"She better not be there," Jeff replied, referring to the house party they were going to as soon as they dropped me off. "She knows we're done."

"She won't take no for an answer, that one," Rick said.

"He speaks from experience," Greg added, facing forward again.

Everyone knew the story. Penny dated my brother for three months the year before, but when she got too lovey-dovey he broke it off with her. She wouldn't stop calling him though. Then she had a minor mental breakdown and lost a lot of weight before her parents finally admitted her to the hospital. She was out of school for a month.

This year, she'd set her sights on Jeff and they'd had a brief fling a few weeks ago. Now he was avoiding her and everyone said he had a thing for some girl in the eleventh grade who just broke up with her longtime boyfriend. I heard he went off to college in September, joined a fraternity and decided he didn't want to be tied down anymore. She was heartbroken and Jeff wanted to step in and lift her spirits.

We all knew what that meant.

I felt sorry for her. I also felt sorry for Penny, who kept getting her heart stomped on and would probably end up in the hospital again. From where I stood at the sidelines, it seemed obvious that she should steer clear of the football team and maybe join the science club instead, but girls just didn't seem to go for guys like me who were good at math. They liked big muscles and stardom. Even if it was only small town stardom.

We drove past the Johnson's hayfield and I wondered what the cows thought of the dust cloud we were creating as we sped up the gravel road.

When at last our large white house came into view at the top of the hill, Rick didn't slow down and I wondered how he was going to make the turn onto our tree-lined driveway.

That was the moment I spotted Francis—our eleven-year-old golden lab—charging down the hill to greet us.

Chapter Two

I grabbed hold of the seat in front of me and pulled myself out of my sandwiched position between Jeff and Rob.

"Slow down," I said to Rick. "Francis got loose."

What was he doing out of the house? I wondered. Our parents weren't home. They'd left early that morning to visit my grandmother. Rick was the last one to leave the house and before that I was sure I'd seen Francis asleep on his bed in the family room as I walked out.

"I'm not slowing down," Rick said. "We're already late for the party, thanks to you."

It all seemed to happen in slow motion after that…as I watched Francis gallop down the hill, his ears flopping. The sound of our tires speeding over the packed dirt and gravel was thunderous in my ears.

"I think you better slow down!" I shouted, hitting Rick on the shoulder.

"Shut up," he said. "He's not stupid. He'll stop when he gets closer."

My heart rose up in my throat as our two paths converged. I prayed that Rick was right about Francis knowing enough to stop when he reached the road.

Then *whack*!—the horrendous sound of the vehicle colliding with my dog.

Only then did Rick slam on the brakes. "Shit!"

"Did you just hit your dog?" Jeff asked as the car skidded sideways to a halt and we were all tossed forward in our seats.

"Lemme out!" I cried as I scrambled over Jeff's lap.

Rick was quicker to open his door and leap out to see what had happened.

My whole body burned with terror at the sight of Francis, more than ten yards back, lying still at the edge of the road.

Chapter Three

I ran to Francis as fast as my legs would carry me and dropped to my knees. I laid my hands on his belly, rubbed them over the contours of his ribs and shoulder blades.

"Francis!" I cried, but he didn't move.

Rick shoved me aside. "Move Jesse! Let me check him!"

I was practically hyperventilating as I stood up, only vaguely aware of the other three guys coming to take a look.

"Is he okay?" I asked, while Rick pressed his ear to Francis's chest to listen for a heartbeat. Then he put his fingers to Francis's nose. "Shit!" he shouted. "He's dead."

"What? No! He can't be!" I dropped to my knees again and laid my head on Francis's side. There were no signs of life. I stared at his belly, willing it to rise and fall. I needed to see him breathing, to know it wasn't true.

"Maybe we should take him to the vet!" I pleaded, unable to accept what I knew to be true. "Maybe they can save him!"

"It's too late," Rick said. "He's gone."

The words, spoken so straightforwardly, made my eyes fill up with tears while blood rushed to my head. My temples began to throb.

"Why didn't you slow down?" I demanded to know. "He was running straight for us."

"I didn't think he'd hit us," Rick explained.

"What a stupid dog," Greg said.

"He's not stupid!" I sobbed. Then I stood up and slammed my open palms into Greg's chest to shove him away. He was built like a tank, however, and barely took a step back.

"Settle down," Rick said, hitting me in the shoulder and shoving me.

"This is all your fault!" I cried. "And what was he doing outside? Didn't you shut the door when you left?"

He stared at me for a long moment, then shoved me again. "This isn't my fault. It's *your* fault, jerk, because we wouldn't even be here if Mom didn't force me to drag you along. We wouldn't be late for the party. We'd be there right now, and Francis wouldn't be..."

Thank God he stopped himself, because I don't know what I would have done if he'd finished that sentence. Actually said the word.

Still, to this day, I fantasize about tackling Rick in that moment and punching him in the head.

But my anger was tempered by grief. I felt as if I were dissolving into a thousand pieces. I swung around and sank to my knees again, gathered my beloved dog—we'd had him since I was three years old—into my arms and wept uncontrollably.

"Jesus," Jeff said. "What are we gonna do? We can't just leave him here."

"No," Rick agreed. "We'll have to take him up to the house."

I felt his hand on my shoulder and this time he spoke more gently.

"Come on Jesse. We have to get him off the road. Help me lift him. We'll put him in the car."

I glanced back at my father's blue sedan. "How?" I asked, wiping at my tears with the back of my hand.

"We'll put him in the trunk."

"The trunk?" I replied. "No. He can't be in there alone."

"It's the only way," Rick replied. "We'll cover him with the blanket. Now get up and help me. Guys? You gotta help too. He's gonna be heavy."

Each breath I took was a hellish, shuddering ordeal as I slid my hands under Francis's torso and raised him up. He was limp and it took four of us to carry him to the car. In hindsight, we should have backed the car up closer, but we were all pretty shaken. Well, at least I was shaken, and I can only assume Rick was as well, though he certainly didn't show it. Maybe it was because his friends were there. He seemed more irritated than anything else.

Awkwardly we placed Francis in the trunk and Rick covered him with the green plaid blanket my father always kept on hand in case we got stranded in a snow storm.

"Stop crying," Rick said as he shut the trunk. "It's over now and we can't do anything to change it."

I felt the other guys staring at me as if I was a wimp, but I didn't care. I opened the car door and got into the front seat, forcing the other three to pile into the back together. I'm sure they weren't happy about it, but they had the sense not to object.

Before Rick got in, he went around to the front of the car to check for damage.

"How's it looking?" Jeff asked when Rick got in.

"The fender's dented."

"At least it's just the fender," Greg replied. "You won't even need to tell the insurance company. You can just hammer that out."

Rick started up the engine. This time, he drove slowly as he turned up our driveway and began the long journey up the hill.

I could barely think. I felt like I was floating in cold water, bobbing up and down while waves splashed in my face. I had to suck in great gulps of air whenever I could.

At last we reached the house and everyone got out of the car. I have no memory of the next few minutes. All I recall is sinking down onto the cool grass in our front yard next to Francis while Rick stood over us.

"We have to go," he said. "When Dad gets home, make sure you tell him it was an accident and that Francis came out of nowhere."

"But he didn't," I replied.

"Jesus, he was running like a bat out of hell."

He was just excited to see us, I thought, as I ran my hand over Francis's smooth coat.

"You *better* tell him it was an accident," Rick warned me as he returned to the car, "because you were there, too, and this wouldn't have happened if you weren't."

"I told you to slow down," I insisted.

"No, you didn't."

"Yes, I did."

"It's your word against mine," Rick said, pausing before he got into the car, "and I have witnesses. On top of that, I'm pretty sure you were the last one to leave the house, remember? Mom's always telling you to shut the back door."

It wasn't true. I hadn't left the door open. I was waiting in the car when Rick came out with his gear slung over his shoulder, running late as usual.

I couldn't wait to tell my father the whole story when he got home. And I was going to tell the truth, whether Rick liked it or not.

Chapter Four

I'd always suspected that Rick was my father's favorite. He was his firstborn child after all, my father's namesake—though my father went by Richard.

When you compared Rick and me, I realized it must have been difficult for my mother to pretend I was as special as him because he excelled at everything he did. He was good looking and popular, he played a number of sports equally well, and he possessed a fierce charisma that seemed to put most people in some sort of hypnotic state. Every other person in a room seemed to disappear when Rick walked into it. All eyes turned to him and everyone was mesmerized. He knew all the right things to say, especially to grownups, and everyone who met him was suitably impressed.

'You sure hit a home run with that boy, Richard,' friends of my father would say when they came over to the house—or 'He's going to be a heartbreaker,' women said to my mother at the supermarket.

I suppose I was invisible in the glare of such perfection, but to be honest, I didn't mind because I was a bit of an introvert, which was why I didn't go seeking a spotlight by trying out for sports teams or running for student council. I was quite content to sit quietly in the corner of a room while Rick carried on conversations or told stories that made everyone laugh.

Naturally he was voted most likely to succeed during his senior year of high school—which turned out to be a good prediction because he ended up working in LA as a sports agent, earning millions from celebrity clients.

But that came much later. I shouldn't be skipping ahead when you probably want to know what happened when my parents came home and found me huddled in the front yard with Francis in my arms.

Chapter Five

It was dark by the time they drove up the tree-lined drive. I should have at least gone into the house to get a warmer jacket at some point, because it was late November in Connecticut and near the freezing point on that particular day after the sun went down. But I didn't want to leave Francis, so I sat there shivering in my light windbreaker until the car headlights nearly blinded me.

My mother was first to get out of the car. "Oh my God, what happened?" She strode toward me and crouched down, laid her hand on Francis's shoulder.

"Rick hit him with the car," I explained as my father approached. He'd left the headlights on.

My rage had been boiling up inside me for nearly two hours and I'm not sure what I sounded like. I think I might have achieved more if I'd remained calm and rational, but I was fourteen years old and didn't possess Rick's clever way with people.

"He murdered him!" I shouted.

"Who murdered who?" my father asked with growing concern.

"Rick killed Francis. He drove right into him, even when I told him not to."

"That can't be true," Mom said, looking up at my father who glared down at me with derision. "Rick loves Francis. He would never do something like that. Certainly not intentionally."

"You're not making any sense, Jesse," my father said in his deep, booming voice. "You're upset, which is understandable, but accidents happen."

He knelt down and stroked Francis's head. "Poor boy. How long ago did it happen?"

"A couple of hours," I replied.

"And you've been out here with him all this time?" my mother asked, laying a sympathetic hand on my cheek.

I nodded, grateful for her gentle warmth in light of my father's severity.

She looked down at Francis and rubbed his side. I could see her eyes tearing up.

"Did he suffer at all?" she asked.

"I don't think so," I replied. "It happened really fast. As soon as we got out of the car, Rick said he was dead."

My father's eyes lifted and he regarded me from beneath those bushy dark brows. "How did he get loose? Did you leave the door open again?"

"No! I swear I didn't! It was Rick! It had to have been."

My parents exchanged a look and I knew they didn't believe me.

"Well," my mother said gently, "whatever happened, we can't change it now and we can't bring Francis back. This was a terrible accident, Jesse, but you mustn't punish yourself. It's no one's fault."

Why did everyone seem to think it was *me*? That *I* was the one who had something to answer for?

"Yes, it *is* someone's fault," I argued. "It's Rick's, because he was driving."

"Now, see here," my father scolded. "I won't hear talk like that. If Francis got out of the house, it could have happened to any of us. It was an accident and if I hear you say otherwise to your brother, you'll have to answer to me. He must feel guilty enough as it is. Do you understand?"

"But it *was* his fault," I pleaded. "He was driving too fast and I told him to slow down but he wouldn't."

My father's eyes darkened. "Did you not hear what I just said to you?"

I'd been raised to respect and obey my father—and to fear him. We all did, even Mom. So I nodded to indicate that yes, I'd heard what he said.

That didn't mean I had to believe he was right.

Chapter Six

Rick didn't come home that night. He slept at Greg's so it was left to me to help Dad bury Francis at the edge of the yard under the big oak tree. My mother suggested the spot because it was visible from the top floor windows of the house, and I agreed it was the right place.

It was ten o'clock by the time we finished. I was so exhausted afterwards, I went straight to bed, but I hardly slept a wink all night. What happened that day had been a terrible ordeal and I couldn't stop replaying all the vivid images in my mind: Francis bounding down the hill to greet us; the sound of our car striking him; then finally the eerie sight of my father shoveling dirt on top of him while I held the flashlight.

I imagined we must have hit Francis in the head with the car, which was why he died so quickly. At least, if that was the case, he probably felt no pain.

That thought provided me with some comfort, though I couldn't overcome the white-hot rage I felt every time I remembered how Rick stood over me in the yard blaming me for what happened.

That perhaps was the real reason I couldn't sleep. My body was on fire with adrenaline, and I wanted to hit something.

Chapter Seven

I woke late the next morning, having finally drifted off into a deep slumber sometime before dawn. Sleepily, I rose from bed, used the washroom, and padded downstairs to the kitchen in my pajamas.

"Mom?"

My voice never echoed back to me in the kitchen before and the implications of that fact caused a lump to form in my throat.

"Mom? Dad? Is anyone here?"

When no answer came, I went to the front hall and looked out the window. Both cars were parked in the driveway, which meant Rick had come home.

"Rick?" I climbed the stairs to check his room, but it was empty and the bed was made.

Suddenly it occurred to me where everyone must be and a feeling of panic swept over me. I hurried to the window in Rick's room, which looked out over the back field and apple orchard, and sure enough, there they were, my mother, father and Rick, all standing over Francis's grave.

I had no idea what was going on out there, but I felt very left out. Without bothering to get dressed, I hurried downstairs, pulled on a pair of rain boots and a jacket, and ran out the back door.

It was not one of my finer moments. I will admit that. When I reached my family, I shouted at all of them accusingly.

"What are you doing out here? Why didn't you wake me?"

My mother turned and looked at me with concern. "You seemed so tired last night, Jesse. I thought you could use some extra sleep."

"If this is Francis's funeral," I said, "I should be here."

"It's not his funeral," my father informed me, impatiently. "Rick just got home and he wanted to see where we buried Francis."

"He was my dog, too," Rick said with a frown, as if I was being selfish.

Maybe I was, but I was only fourteen and I was grief-stricken and angry.

"Come here," Rick said, holding out his hand to wave me closer.

I slowly approached.

"I was thinking," Rick said, "that we should get some sort of monument. Maybe a small headstone. I have enough in my savings account to pay for it."

"That would be a fine gesture, Rick," my father said, "but please let me cover the cost."

Rick laid a hand on my shoulder. "What do you think we should have engraved on it?" he asked. "His name of course, but maybe we should come up with some sort of epitaph."

I thought about it for a moment. "What about: Here lies Francis, beloved dog and best friend?"

My voice shook and I didn't think I could speak again without breaking down.

"That sounds perfect," Rick said. He looked down at me meaningfully. "I'm really sorry, Jesse. I don't think I'll ever be able to forgive myself."

He closed his eyes and pinched the bridge of his nose, as if he, too, could not speak about it anymore.

My father squeezed his shoulder and patted him on the back.

Chapter Eight

Five years later

"Hey, Bentley. Where's your leash?"

Bentley's head lifted, his ears perked up and he jumped off the sofa in the family room. I rose from my chair at the kitchen table and headed for the laundry room. With tail wagging, Bentley followed me in.

Dad waited only a month after we lost Francis before coming home one afternoon with a brand new puppy—an adorable black lab I fell in love with at first sight.

From that moment on, Bentley and I were best pals. He formed a closer bond with me than anyone else because both my parents worked and I was the first one home every afternoon to take him for a walk. I made sure his food and water bowls were always full in the mornings, and he slept on the floor in my room on a large green pillow. I loved him dearly.

After attaching the leash to Bentley's collar, I led him out the front door. While I stood there locking the door behind me, I heard a car speed by on the road at the bottom of the hill. A few years earlier, a crew had come in and paved the road all the way to the next town, so we now had a steadier stream of traffic moving at a faster clip in front of our house. In addition to that, a number of new homes had gone up since the paving project was announced. We were no longer the only house between the main road and the bootlegger's shack—which as far as I knew was still there.

There had been other changes to our lives as well. Rick graduated from high school with honors and received a scholarship to UCLA. He was still there, living out west, working on an MBA.

As for me, I was still living at home, working at the airport as an operations assistant until I figured out what to do with my life. My father wanted me to enroll in a science program and go to dental or medical school. I certainly had the grades for either of those options, but I just wasn't that keen on following in my father's footsteps. We were different, he and I, and I wanted to choose my own path. Maybe it would have something to do with aviation. I'd always had an interest in that. I just wasn't sure yet.

That's when I met Angela. She, too, had decided to take a year off after high school and she was working as a waitress in one of the airport restaurants. Just like seeing Bentley for the first time, it was love at first sight when she approached me in the staff parking lot, needing help because she'd locked herself out of her car. I called AAA for her and waited for them to arrive, but when she finally got into her car, the engine wouldn't start. So after arranging to have her vehicle towed to a repair shop, I gave her a lift home.

Three weeks later, we were seeing each other every day and I was head over heels in love. I hadn't had much experience with girls and I never imagined it could be like that, but everything about Angela suited me. She was a bit of a math geek, like me, and she hadn't had much experience in the dating scene either. I couldn't understand why, because I thought she was the most beautiful creature to ever walk the earth. Her hair was jet black, cut in a shoulder-length bob with bangs, and she had giant brown eyes and a soft, smooth ivory complexion. She was very petite at five-foot-three and went to yoga class three times a week. Every time I saw her, I felt like I'd been run over by a truck. She was fun and sweet and incredibly kindhearted. Bentley loved her, too.

Before long I started thinking about moving out of my parents' house and getting a place of my own. My parents didn't approve, of course, because they still wanted me to go to university and make something of myself.

When I brought it up at the dinner table one night, my father's bushy eyebrows pulled together and two large vertical creases formed between them. He set down his fork and knife and leaned back in his chair.

"How will you ever go to a good school if you're tied down to some waitress here in town, struggling to pay your rent every month?" he asked.

"Maybe I don't want to go to a good school," I defiantly replied. "Maybe I just want to keep working at the airport." My mother fidgeted uncomfortably and her eyes pleaded for me to walk away from this one.

He scoffed at me, as if I were a fool. "Believe me, when the shine wears off of this exciting new relationship and you're stuck in a dead end job, arguing with that girl about how you're going to pay the phone bill, you'll feel differently, and you'll wish you had listened to me."

"Maybe so," I replied, "but it's my life and I'm not a kid anymore. I'm nineteen and you have to let me make my own decisions."

He and Mom exchanged a look, as if they were carrying on a mental conversation I wasn't privileged to be a part of.

Then Mom leaned across the table and clasped my hand. "Jesse, it's not that we don't like Angela. She's probably a very nice girl. But you've had so little experience in that area. How can I say this...?" She paused, then continued. "It's important to try on some different styles and sizes before you make a commitment you can't get yourself out of."

She was so much gentler than my father. Nevertheless, I frowned at her. "It's not like we're moving in together." Though the idea wasn't far from my mind. Angela and I had only been seeing each other for a month, but I figured—and hoped—moving in would be the next step. For now, I just wanted a place where I could have my privacy to be with her.

My father still hadn't picked up his fork. "Your mother's right," he said in that deep, reverberating voice that made everyone quiver. "You should be dating lots of girls before you settle for just one."

"Like Rick does?" I tersely asked. I set my fork down and leaned back in my chair. "He dates all kinds of girls and manages to have a whale of a time. Do you want me to be more like him and break lots of hearts?"

"That's not fair," Mom said. "Rick has always worked very hard at school and sports. He's incredibly busy and doesn't have time for a serious relationship, that's all."

"And look where he is now," my father added. "In the MBA program at Anderson Business School. He'll have his pick of high-paying jobs the minute he steps off that campus."

I took a deep breath and let it out because I knew this conversation was pointless. My parents wanted me to be a great "success" like Rick, but when it came right down to it, my definition of success differed from theirs. I didn't need to make a million dollars. I didn't want to have a series of superficial relationships with girls I had nothing in common with. I'd already found the girl who was right for me and I just wanted to be with her. It didn't mean I was going to give up any thought of doing something more with my life. I just wanted her at my side, no matter what I chose to do.

"It's my decision to make," I said, pulling my napkin from my lap and tossing it onto the table. "Excuse me, Mom. I'm finished now."

My father stared up at me with displeasure as I carried my plate to the kitchen. "Fine," he said, "but don't expect any help from me when you can't pay your rent."

"I'll remember that." On my way upstairs, I picked up the newspaper from the front hall so I could check out the classifieds.

Chapter Nine

A week later, I signed the lease on my first apartment, which came cheap because it was a mile from the airport and the roar of the planes flying overhead turned off most prospective renters. It was convenient for me, however, because I could reach work in ten minutes by bicycle, and Angela could come and stay over anytime she liked.

My dad was true to his word. He didn't help me with anything. He didn't let me take any of the furniture from my room—not a single item—so I had to purchase a bed and a table at yard sales. My mother couldn't stand with me on this, but I remember the lump in my throat when she quietly slipped fifty dollars into my hand on the day I moved out.

It was Angela who helped me shop for plates and kitchen utensils, bedding and a small television set, all of which we found at second hand stores. Her parents gave me a sofa they wanted to get rid of anyway.

Ironically, the one thing my father let me take from the house was the only thing I really wanted.

He let me have Bentley.

I didn't call my parents or speak to them for over two months. I wasn't trying to punish them. I just had no interest in being lectured about why I was making the worst mistake of my life. So I waited it out and thought maybe, eventually, they would accept my decision and let me choose my own path.

The way I saw it, even if I *was* making a mistake, it was *my* mistake to make, and I was ready and willing to learn from it—and all the others I would likely make in the coming years.

Wasn't that part of life? To follow your heart? Explore the unknown and engage in a little trial and error?

Angela, for the most part, agreed with me, though she worried about me losing touch with my family. She certainly didn't want to feel responsible for that, so when a third month passed and there was still no communication, she suggested I pick up the phone.

"Call when you know your father won't be there," she suggested one evening while we were out walking Bentley. "How much you want to bet your mom will be thrilled to hear your voice and she won't even tell him you called if you don't want her to."

I considered that. "If she wants to hear my voice, she could call me any time," I said. "I'm in the book."

"No, you're not. You won't be in the book until the next one comes out."

"When will that be?" I asked.

"I have no idea," she replied with a chuckle.

Bentley paused briefly to lift a leg and pee on a telephone pole, then continued on.

"I'm sure Mom knows the number for directory assistance," I mentioned.

Playfully, Angela shoved me into the chain-link fence that ran along the sidewalk. "You're impossible," she said.

I bounced off the fence and returned to her side. "Yep, and that's why you love me."

"Is it?" she replied with mischief in her eyes. "I thought it was for another reason entirely."

I smiled and wrapped my arm around her. We walked on, our steps in perfect unison while a giant Boeing 767 passed over our heads—taking off for some exotic location, no doubt.

The thought of what unexplored territories were over my own horizon filled me with hope and excitement. I felt like one those jetliners, finally lifting off the runway. Everything in my world seemed new and full of promise.

It's a shame that feeling didn't last longer. Two weeks later I was forced to come down from the clouds when my mother called with some news.

Suddenly, I was back on the ground, living among the pressures of my old world.

Chapter Ten

The sound of her voice on the phone caught me off guard because I'd just stepped out of the shower. I was dripping wet and wrapped in a towel. Angela was asleep in my bed, tangled in the sheets, wearing my flannel pajama bottoms and an oversized T-shirt.

As I carried the phone out of the bedroom, I had to drag the long cord over Bentley on his giant green pillow. He lifted his head and tilted it to the side as he watched me.

"Mom, it's nice to hear from you," I said.

It was a polite response, but it was also the truth. The sound of my mother's voice in my ear reduced me to my ten-year-old self, to a time when she was my whole world. Yet that seemed like a lifetime ago.

For some unknown reason, I felt a sudden rush of panic. Had there been some horrible family tragedy? Did someone die? Was that why she was calling so early in the morning?

To this day, I don't know why I thought that, but it woke me up to something. I regretted not picking up the phone sooner as Angela had so often encouraged me to do.

"I'm so glad I caught you," Mom said cheerfully. I let out a breath of relief knowing no one had died. She simply missed me. I could hear it in her voice.

"How are you getting along?" she asked. "Are you eating enough vegetables?"

I laughed. "Yes, Mom. I'm eating well."

"And how's Bentley? The house is so quiet here with both of you gone."

"I imagine it is," I replied. "Bentley's doing great. I come home for lunch every day, so he's never alone for too long."

I waited for her to ask about Angela, but there was a long noteworthy silence.

"How's Dad?" I asked.

"Oh, you know, busy as usual. His receptionist is retiring next month, so he's looking for someone."

"Ah."

There was another pause.

"You should come over for dinner sometime," Mom said. "Bring your girlfriend."

"Angela," I mentioned.

"Yes, Angela..." Another pause. "Is she still working at the airport pub?"

My mother was doing her best to sound friendly and accepting, but I could hear her disapproval and disappointment not far beneath her cheerful façade. No doubt she and Dad would have preferred me to date a law student. Or even a flight attendant, for that matter. At least flight attendants wore heels and blazers.

"Yeah," I replied. "She's making great tips."

Bentley appeared at my feet and panted up at me. I reached down to rub behind his ears.

"That's wonderful," Mom said.

A plane flew overhead; there was some static on the line, and I wondered if my mother was still on the other end.

NEW MADRID COUNTY LIBRARY
309 E. MAIN ST.
PORTAGEVILLE, MO 63873

"Rick's coming home for a few weeks over Christmas," she said, breaking the silence at last. "Will you be coming home, too?"

It seemed an odd question, and I combed my fingers through my wet hair. "You mean like...to sleep?"

To wake up Christmas morning and open Santa's gifts as a family?

"Your room is still here," she said. "You can come home any time you like."

I nodded. "That's nice to know, Mom. Thanks."

Maybe I was being too presumptuous, assuming that my parents expected me to fail—even *wanted* me to—so that they could say 'I told you so' and wrestle me back onto the right track.

Was it possible they had changed their minds and were ready to accept the choices I was making?

That would be nice—if they could simply pick me up and dust me off if I stumbled, instead of insisting that I not stumble in the first place.

"I don't have a lot of time right now, Mom," I said. "I have to get to work, and Bentley needs to go outside. Maybe we can talk later. When is Rick coming home?"

"He's flying in on the fifth," she replied. "Maybe you'll be the one to haul his suitcase off the plane. That's what you do at your job, isn't it?"

I closed my eyes and tipped my head back against the wall. "Yeah, Mom. That's what I do."

I said good-bye and hung up. When I finally made it to work and began loading baggage onto a Bombardier CRJ-200, I glanced up at the pilots in the flight deck windows and imagined for the thousandth time what it would feel like to fly such an incredible machine.

Perhaps a career in aviation was in my future, but I was nevertheless determined not to let my parents pressure me into any career before I was ready. Even if it was a career of my own choosing.

Chapter Eleven

Though I didn't speak to my father at all over the next few weeks, I did hear from Mom who called to tell me Rick's flight number and what time it would arrive on the fifth. She asked if I would meet him at the gate because she and Dad would be at work. She also asked if I wanted to come for turkey dinner on Christmas Day.

"Bring Angela, of course," she added.

Encouraged by the fact that she had remembered Angela's name this time, I accepted her invitation.

I wasn't scheduled to work on the day Rick's flight came in, so I was able to meet him at the gate. After we found each other in the terminal, I asked him about school and LA. He then asked about my job and the new apartment.

"You should show it to me now," he said, "before I go to Mom and Dad's. I can't believe my baby brother's all grown up."

He teasingly messed my hair as we stepped onto the escalator. I elbowed him in the ribs.

"Fine," I said, "but you'll have to take a cab unless you want to hop on the back of my bike with your suitcase. Or you could walk. It's only a mile or two."

"You ride a bike to work?" Rick asked, his head drawing back slightly.

"Yeah. Saves on gas. And car payments."

I walked with him to where the taxis were lined up outside, gave my address to one of the drivers, then told Rick that I'd meet him at my place in a few minutes. I fetched my bike, hopped on and managed to peddle fast enough to beat him to my front door.

"It's a great spot," Rick said after I gave him a two-minute tour of my apartment, "if you don't mind airplanes landing in your front yard. Geez, how do you sleep through that?"

"I hardly notice," I told him. "And Bentley doesn't seem to mind it."

Rick glanced around skeptically. "I don't know. I don't think I could take it." He flopped onto his back on my sofa and crossed his legs at the ankles. "It's great to be here, though. We should go do something."

"Like what?" This was a new development: my brother wanting to spend time with me in a public place. I couldn't remember a single instance when he didn't resent being forced by Mom and Dad to let me tag along with him somewhere.

"I don't know," he said. "I'm starving. They didn't serve anything on the plane except for pretzels. We should get some lunch."

"Sure," I replied, "but if you want to go downtown we'll have to take the bus."

"No problem," he said, rising to his feet. "Let's go."

Rick and I enjoyed a late lunch with a few beers at a downtown pub, and before I realized what I was saying, I was telling him about my plans to look into flight school.

"Makes sense," he said, raising his beer to his lips and taking a sip. "You were always into rockets and planes when you were a kid. What do Mom and Dad think?"

I glanced at the waitress loading up her tray at the bar. "I haven't mentioned it to them."

"Why not?"

"Because we don't talk much," I replied, "and even if we did, I don't think I could stomach giving Dad that much satisfaction. He might think I was doing it just to make him happy."

Rick laughed. "Well, that wouldn't do, because we all know how much you enjoy being a total disappointment."

I shook my head at him, choosing not to argue because we both knew it was true, to some extent. Nevertheless, I didn't appreciate that he felt compelled to point it out.

"I'm only joking." Rick signaled to the waitress to bring him another beer.

I finished the last of my salad, wiped my mouth with the napkin and laid it on the table. "Wonder what they'll think of Angela when they meet her."

"They haven't met her yet?" Rick asked with surprise.

"No, but Mom invited us for dinner Christmas Day, so you'll get to witness all the subtle digs and backhanded compliments."

"Maybe they'll surprise you," Rick said.

"Maybe so," I replied, "but I'm not holding my breath. And listen, don't mention flight school to them. I still haven't made up my mind and I don't want Dad to get out his conductor's wand and start directing the show. If I go, I'll pay for it myself, and I'll go when I'm good and ready."

"Sure."

The waitress brought Rick's third beer and I asked him what he was planning to give to Mom and Dad for Christmas—I had no idea what to get them and I wanted to change the subject.

He said he had a couple of hardcovers in mind. Then he asked me what I was planning to give Angela.

Looking back on it, I should have told him it was none of his business. And I never should have taken her to dinner Christmas Day.

Chapter Twelve

I often wondered, growing up, what it was about my brother that was so seductive to women. He was good looking—that was a given—but it didn't explain why they all seemed to melt into a puddle of sticky goo when he engaged them in a conversation about something as simple as the weather.

I suppose he was born with some sort of rare, penetrating charisma that few of us are blessed with. It's why he later went on to make millions in his profession. He could convince anyone—men and women alike—to say yes to anything. 'Another two million per year for that rookie outfielder? Sure, Mr. Fraser. We'd love to pay that.'

When Rick and I returned to my apartment after lunch, I was surprised to find Angela sitting on the sofa with Bentley, watching television. As soon as we walked through the door, she hit the mute button on the remote and stood up.

"Hey," I said, shrugging out of my jacket. "What are you doing here?"

"I'm on my lunch break," she replied. "I have to go back in half an hour."

I gestured toward Rick who walked in behind me. "This is my brother, Rick. Rick, this is Angela."

"Hi." She waved at him. "It's great to finally meet you."

"You, too." He moved forward to shake her hand, then he took a seat on the upholstered chair across from the TV. "So you guys met at work?"

"Yeah." Angela sat down again and told the story of how she locked her keys in her car and I came to her rescue like a knight in shining armor.

Rick then asked what high school she went to. When she told him which one, he asked if she knew so-and-so, because Rick knew everyone. They chatted for a while about their mutual acquaintances.

I went to use the washroom and when I returned, they were talking about Angela's yoga classes, and Rick was interested in trying a class for himself.

As soon as I stepped into view she checked her watch and stood up. "Geez, I'm going to be late. Wish I could stay but I have to go."

She hurried toward me and gave me a quick kiss on the cheek. "I'll see you guys later. Bye, Bentley."

With that, she was out the door.

"Cute girl," Rick said, slouching low in his chair. "How long have you been dating her?"

"A few months," I replied.

He nodded with approval as he pulled off his sneakers and settled in to watch some television. "Nice work. I'm sure you have nothing to worry about. Mom and Dad will think she's great."

"I'm not worried," I informed him.

Because it didn't matter to me what they thought. It only mattered how Angela and I felt about each other.

It's unfortunate that I didn't know, at the time, that there would be other far worse things to worry about, and none of them would involve my parents. Maybe if I had known, I might have been able to prevent the worst of them from happening.

Or maybe not. I've come to learn that certain things in life are beyond our control.

Others are beyond comprehension.

Chapter Thirteen

The turkey dinner on Christmas Day went surprisingly well. Angela, Bentley, and I arrived at my parent's house around noon and my father was friendly and welcoming.

It was a side of him I had seen many times before. He was an impeccable host when guests crossed his threshold, whoever they were.

After we finished dessert and coffee, Angela offered to help Mom clear off the table and wash the dishes.

"Thank you, Angela," Mom said. "What an angel you are."

I offered to help as well, but Mom insisted that I remain in the dining room to sip Madeira with Rick and Dad. The only thing missing was a box of Havana cigars.

"So Jesse," Dad said, leaning back in his chair at the head of the table. "Rick tells me you're planning to enroll in flight school. When is the application deadline?"

My gaze shot to Rick's and he winced apologetically. "Sorry," he said, "it slipped out."

I took a swig of the port, which was too sweet for my taste, but in that particular moment, it didn't really matter.

"I haven't made up my mind," I replied. "I'm considering it, that's all. Keeping all my options open."

My father's eyes narrowed as he studied me intently. "Programs like that are competitive," he said. "You can't sit around thinking about it. It's been awhile since you sat in a classroom. The longer you wait, the harder it will be."

"I've never had problems in a classroom before," I told him. "I'm sure I'll manage."

"You have to do more than just *manage*," he replied. "You have to take the bull by the horns."

Dad continued to regard me with expectation and when I gave no reply, he leaned forward. "It's a good career choice, son. And remember you can come to me if you need help with tuition fees or living expenses. When the time comes."

I may have possessed a stubborn, independent streak, but I wasn't a fool. "Thanks Dad," I said. "I appreciate that. I'll let you know if I decide to apply."

Dad nodded and turned his attention to Rick. "So tell me more about the sports agency where you've been interning. What sort of clients do they represent?"

The direction of the spotlight shifted to my brother, as it always did, and I relaxed back in my chair.

After we finished sipping the port, I volunteered to go outside and collect some kindling from the woodpile so Dad could light a fire in the living room fireplace.

"Let's go, Bentley," I said, giving a whistle as I made my way through the kitchen where Angela and Mom were finishing up the dishes. He rose from his place on the rug and trotted out the back door behind me.

A light snow had fallen—just a small dusting of white across the fields. There was still some light in the sky, enough for me to toss a ball for Bentley and let him run back and forth into the orchard a few times.

A short while later, with a heavy load of firewood in my arms, I walked back into the house. But as I entered the kitchen from the mud room, I halted in my tracks at the sight of Angela opening a bottle of beer she had just pulled out of the fridge, and handing it to Rick.

The glimmer of flirtation I saw in her eyes was unmistakable, as was the manner in which Rick smiled back at her with that wolfish look I had seen many times in the past. With so many different girls.

Bentley trotted past me to lap up some water from his bowl by the stove. Angela's eyes caught mine and everything about her demeanor changed. Her brows lifted.

"Hey, you want a beer? Looks like your parents stocked the fridge just for us."

"Sure," I replied. "Let me get rid of this firewood first."

Rick casually leaned back against the counter and took a swig from his bottle, intently watching me carry the wood into the living room.

"Rick," I said later in the kitchen while Angela was talking to Mom in the living room.

"Yeah?" He pulled a bag of chips out of the cupboard and ripped it open.

"I need you to stay away from her." I didn't see the point in mincing words, and I knew I hadn't imagined what I saw. "She's not like other girls."

Rick stared at me as if I'd grown a second head. "What are you talking about?"

"I'm talking about Angela. Stay away from her. Don't flirt with her. Just try to imagine that she's your sister because she might be that someday."

His lips parted and he rubbed at his forehead. "I think I know what you're saying, and it's really pissing me off."

I sucked in a breath, but no words came.

Rick laid the chip bag down on the counter. "Are you suggesting…?" He paused. "Are you suggesting that I was trying to flirt with your girl? Seriously, Jesse? You're my *brother*. I'm home for a couple of weeks, that's it, and you want to pick a fight with me? Is that what this is? Jesus. She's not even my type. No offense." He held up a hand. "She's great. She's really cute and everything, but I'm not into poaching my baby brother's girlfriends." He frowned at me. "Are you serious?"

"Yeah, dead serious." I wasn't going to let him convince me that I imagined it. I knew what I saw.

He leaned back against the counter and regarded me steadily. "Let's just pretend this conversation never happened, all right?"

"No," I replied. "I don't want to pretend anything. Stay away from her or I'll knock your teeth out."

I had never said anything like that to Rick before and I could tell by the way he was looking at me—by the way the color drained from his face—that I'd shocked him.

"I think you're losing it," he said with concern.

But what was he concerned for, exactly? His safety? Or my sanity? Should I have been concerned as well?

"You know I'd never do that to you," he added. "You're my brother."

For a moment I wondered if maybe I *was* crazy. Maybe I was still angry about what happened that day years ago when he struck and killed Francis out front on the road.

Maybe I was jealous because he was everything to my parents and I was nothing.

Maybe I was paranoid and believed I truly did become invisible whenever he was around. And I didn't want to become invisible to Angela.

I struggled to wrestle my anger under control and chose not to say anything more.

Rick moved past me and patted my shoulder reassuringly.

Something in me relaxed. I was at least glad I had confronted him.

I only wish I'd had the sense to find the proper way to confront Angela, too.

Chapter Fourteen

After a three-and-a-half-week winter vacation at home, it was time for Rick to return to California for his final semester at UCLA. He caught a flight out on New Year's Day.

I felt guilty when I said good-bye to him at the airport, outside the entrance to security. Since the family dinner on Christmas Day—when I'd accused him of flirting with my girlfriend—nothing had been the same between us. A wedge had come down like a meat cleaver that night and we hardly saw each other for the rest of the holidays. He didn't call to spend time with me, and when I called the house, he was never home. The few times I did see him, there was no more brotherly teasing, no more headlocks and noogies.

I was accustomed to a cool distance and lack of communication between me and my parents, but suddenly I was facing that same guarded expression from my brother, and I began to wonder if the problem was with *me*.

Did I feel some sort of contempt for every member of my family? Did they sense it and respond as any normal person would? If you believed someone disliked you, wouldn't you withdraw from them? If they treated you with mistrust, wouldn't you give up trying to be close?

Was that why I was estranged from my family? Was it *me*?

So I made an extra effort to hug Rick a little tighter than usual at the airport on the day he left.

"I'm sorry about what happened on Christmas Day," I said quickly in his ear. "Let's forget about it, okay?"

We stepped back and a look of relief washed over his face. "No apologies," he said. "She's a great girl. You were right to be possessive, and if I did anything out of line, I apologize. You know me. I can't help trying to charm the girls."

I chuckled and looked down at my shoes. "Maybe you should go to flirting rehab."

He laughed, too. "Yeah. And listen, hang onto that one," he said as he started to back away. "She's a keeper."

I looked up. "Don't flunk out when you get back to class," I said.

"I'll try not to." He turned and waved a hand over his shoulder. Then he was gone, and I experienced a sudden pang of loss as a vivid memory flashed through my mind…of Rick and me building a snowman in front of our house. I was only five or six. He helped me push a giant snowball up the slope of the driveway.

As I turned away from the entrance to security and walked through the wide corridors of the airport, another random memory came to me. I remembered a night when our parents had gone out and left us home without a babysitter for the first time. We ate too much junk food and an hour after we went to bed, I woke up with a stomach ache. Rick fetched me a glass of water and stayed at my side, assuring me it would pass. The sick feeling did pass, and eventually I fell asleep.

He was a good brother when we were children. Now he was gone and somehow I knew he would never return to the east coast to live. Life would carry us in different directions. I would remain here while he would pursue a career in California. And of course he would be wildly successful.

Little did I know that I would see him again far sooner than I expected.

Chapter Fifteen

A few days after Rick left, I began to detect subtle changes in Angela's personality. She went to bed earlier, grew less talkative, and seemed to have lost the quirky sense of humor I found so attractive.

Depression wasn't something people discussed as often or as openly back then, but even if it was, I'm not sure I would have considered it a possibility. All I knew was that my girlfriend had retreated into a shell for some reason I couldn't understand and I missed her. I wanted her back.

"Want to go to a movie tonight?" I asked her on the phone when I arrived home to an empty apartment after work. That was unusual for a Friday. Instead of coming to my place, she had gone to her parent's house.

"Not tonight," she replied. "I'm not feeling that great."

"Is everything okay?" I asked. "Are you sick?" I paused for a moment, then sat on the sofa. "You seem down."

"I'm just tired," she replied. "They've been giving me too many early morning shifts. I think I need to catch up on some sleep."

"All right. Why don't you get some rest and give me a call tomorrow?"

"I will," she replied.

The following day, my phone never rang.

Nor did it ring the day after that.

~

On Monday night, I went to the pub where Angela worked and asked to speak to her. The manager informed me that she had called in sick for the past three days.

As soon as my shift ended, I rode my bike to her parents' house and knocked on the door. Her mother answered.

"Oh, Jesse," she said with a look of sympathy and regret that caught me off guard. "Hi."

I was still out of breath from the long bike ride, and had to wipe my coat sleeve across my brow. "Is Angela here?"

"Yes, she's in her room." Mrs. Donovan stepped back and opened the door wider to invite me in. "Why don't you go in and talk to her? She could use some cheering up."

"Cheering up?" I replied as I stepped over the threshold and removed my sneakers.

Mrs. Donovan sighed. "She hasn't been feeling well for the past few days. I can't get her to eat and she won't go see a doctor. I'm a bit concerned."

"Does she have any other symptoms?" I asked. Not that it would make a difference if Mrs. Donovan recited a list because I wasn't a medical professional. I loaded suitcases on airplanes for a living.

"Do you mean like a sinus infection or nausea?" she asked. "Not that I know of. She just won't get out of bed. I'd like her to have some blood work done because it could be an iron deficiency or something simple like that. Maybe you could talk her into going to see her doctor? She won't listen to me. She keeps telling me she's fine."

"I'll try."

I moved down the hall and knocked on her door. No answer came, so I knocked a second time. Meanwhile my heart began to pound. What if this was something more serious, like cancer or some other fatal ailment?

If that's what we were dealing with we needed to find out sooner rather than later. I knocked harder and more urgently.

Chair legs scraped across the floor inside, followed by the sound of rapid footsteps.

"What is it?" Angela snapped from the other side of the door.

At least she's out of bed, I thought.

"It's me. Jesse."

More silence.

"Can I come in?" I asked.

She certainly took her time thinking about it. I was forced to stand in the hallway while her mother watched me discreetly from the kitchen.

I knew in that moment that something was definitely wrong with my girlfriend. Then the knob slowly turned, and the door opened.

Chapter Sixteen

"Geez, you look like hell," I said when Angela invited me in. Her hair was greasy and matted to her head. She wore a loose pair of gray sweatpants with holes at the knees and a white T-shirt that had seen better days. There was a filmy sheen to her complexion. If I didn't know better, I'd think she hadn't washed her face since Christmas.

"I know," she replied and shut the door behind me.

I moved into the room and glanced around at the unmade bed and the dirty dishes on the nightstand. "You okay?"

"Not really." She sat down on the edge of the bed and dropped her gaze to her hands on her lap. I wondered why she wouldn't look at me.

Crouching down before her, I took both her hands in mine. "What can I do?"

"Nothing."

I paused, then raised her hands to my lips and kissed them. "Your mom wanted me to convince you to go see a doctor. She thinks you might have an iron deficiency."

I certainly wasn't about to say, 'You should get tested because you might have some horrible terminal disease.'

Angela shook her head. "I don't have an iron deficiency."

"Then what is it?" I asked. "Tell me because I want to help. I miss you and I want you to feel better. No matter what it takes, I'm here for you."

Her eyes lifted and she regarded me with dark and angry derision. I felt as if I'd just walked onto the set of *The Exorcist.*

More than a little shaken by this change in the girl I loved, I sat back on the floor and leaned on both arms. "Talk to me."

For a long moment she fiddled with the frayed fabric around the holes of her sweatpants, then she abruptly stood up and walked to the window. Looking out at the neighbor's house next door, she folded her arms at her chest. "It's not an easy thing to say."

"Try," I replied.

Turning to face me, she sat down on the windowsill. "I'm not happy here, and I need to leave. I've already booked a plane ticket, but I haven't told my parents yet."

My brow furrowed with bewilderment. "A plane ticket to where?"

"Out West," she said. "California."

A sick feeling rolled like a jagged boulder into my gut, and I rose to my feet. "Why? What's in California? Or should I ask *who*?"

Suddenly the tension in the room was as thick as bread dough.

"Your brother," she said.

Shutting my eyes, I cupped my forehead in a hand. "No."

"Yes. I'm sorry. I didn't want to hurt you, but it's why I've been curled up in a ball for the past three days. I can't stay here anymore. I'm suffocating, Jesse. I need to go to LA."

"To be with Rick?" I asked, horrified.

She nodded.

"Does he know about this? Does he know how you feel?"

She scoffed and sat down on the bed. "Of course he knows and it's been hell for both of us. We both tried so hard to ignore how we felt, but it just wasn't possible. I'm in love with him and I have to be with him."

The room was spinning. Everything was turning red.

"What are you telling me?" I asked. "That the two of you went around together behind my back?"

Gaze lowered, she nodded.

"When?" I demanded to know.

How could I not have known?

Angela shrugged. "Usually while you were at work. Sometimes we met at your place."

No, no.

No! This was too much!

Bracing my hands on my hips, I began to pace around her bedroom. "For the love of God, please don't tell me you slept with him."

Her lack of a response provided the answer and sent my blood into a wild frenzy. I stopped pacing and faced her. "Are you crazy? He doesn't love you, not like I do."

How pathetic I sounded. I wanted to smother myself with a pillow.

Angela rose defensively to her feet. "Yes, he does. You don't know what you're talking about. You don't know what it was like." She paused to catch her breath. "I'm sorry, but I'm in love with him and I can't take this anymore. Ever since he left, I've been wasting away. I'll die if I don't go. I need to be with him and I'm leaving tomorrow."

I shook my head in a mad attempt to clear this nightmare from my brain. It couldn't be happening. Rick wouldn't have done this to me.

Had he really lied to me at the terminal when we said goodbye? How could he have made me feel like such a jealous fool?

"Have you talked to him since he left?" I asked. "Does he know you want to follow him?"

"Of course he knows," she replied. "He told me to come and move in with him because he can't take it either. You don't understand. What happened between us was..." She stopped.

"It was *what*?" My stomach churned. I was going to be sick.

"It was intense and I can't possibly explain it any better than that. You wouldn't understand. There are no words. All I know is that I never felt anything like this before and I believe he's my soul mate. I think we must have known each other in heaven or something, and I think it's why I met you in the parking lot that day. You were meant to lead me to Rick. That's why it all happened this way."

I seriously wanted to puke.

Soul mate? They met in heaven? She had completely lost her mind.

"It won't last," I told her. "It may seem exciting and romantic now, but I know my brother. Mark my words, you'll end up with a broken heart."

She shook her head again. "No, you're wrong. I know he's been with a lot of girls—he told me about all that—but this is different. I'm not like the other girls who go after him, and he needs me as much as I need him. I feel terrible that this is hurting you, Jesse. Believe me, he feels terrible, too. But we have to be together."

The rage I felt toward my brother paled in comparison to the dismal despair that was snaking its way through my body. I loved Angela with a passion I never knew existed, and the thought of losing her to my brother made me want to double over in agony.

I couldn't even begin to imagine that she had made love to him. That she had given herself to him so completely. I wanted to collapse to my knees and beg her to tell me it wasn't true.

"Please, Angela," I said. "Don't do this." I took a step closer. "He's not the one for you. I love you and I'll marry you tomorrow if you'll stay. Please, don't go."

I had never in my life felt so wretched and pathetic.

She backed away. "Don't touch me. I'm not yours anymore. I'm his."

God in heaven. I wanted to wring his neck. My hands clenched into fists. I couldn't breathe…Couldn't get air into my lungs.

"I'm sorry," Angela said. "We didn't want to hurt you, but we couldn't stop it. We *tried*."

That was enough. It was more than I could take. I had to get out of there.

"Good luck to you both," I said, knowing they would eventually be miserable together—although Rick wouldn't let that go on for long. The minute the shine wore off, he'd cut Angela loose and enjoy his freedom again like he always did.

Meanwhile Angela would wallow in despair for months or years.

If she thought *this* was bad, just wait.

"Bye," I said as I turned and walked out of her room.

Out of her house and out of her life.

I peddled home through the frigid, murderous cold, as if the hounds of hell were behind me.

When I climbed into bed that night, I imagined what the future would hold for Angela. What would I do when she came home in tears six months from now after Rick broke her heart and moved on to some other girl? Would I be here to comfort her? Would I take her back?

I rolled to my side and stared at the wall. My chest felt heavy. What if it turned out differently? What if Rick really did love her and she was the one who would change him forever?

What if *someday* I was uncle to Angela's children?

I wasn't sure which scenario would be worse.

And either way, would I ever be able to forgive?

Chapter Seventeen

Someday came sooner than I expected. Five months after I said good-bye to Angela and stood on the tarmac watching her flight take off for LA—five months after I promised myself I would forget her—I received a phone call out of the blue.

"Hi, Jesse."

The sound of her voice in my ear caused a fireball of grief to explode in my stomach. I couldn't speak right away. All I could do was plunk down on a chair in the kitchen and rest my elbows on my knees.

"Are you there?" she asked.

"Yeah, I'm here." I closed my eyes and raked a hand through my hair.

Why was she calling? To tell me she and Rick were getting married?

Or to tell me he'd cheated on her and she wanted to come home?

It still pains me to admit it, but I wanted desperately for the latter to be true. I wanted her to tell me she missed me and that she'd made a terrible mistake. Rick wasn't the man she believed him to be. I wanted to hear, 'Please, Jesse, I'm miserable. Will you give me a second chance?'

Would I, if she asked?

But that wasn't why she was calling.

"You must be surprised to hear from me," she said.

"Yeah." I leaned back in my chair and stared up at the ceiling. "How are you doing?"

There was a long pause. Then she sighed. "I'm not sure. It all depends on the next couple of weeks."

"What do you mean?" I asked.

When she didn't elaborate, I had to poke and prod. "Are you going to tell me what this is about? Or did you just call to torture me?"

Her voice became a whisper. "Jesse, I'm really sorry. You know that was never my intention."

My pride bucked and I shook my head. "Don't worry about it. Really. Forget I said that. What do you want, Angela? Why are you calling?"

And that's when she dropped the bomb.

"You're *what*?" I slowly stood up.

"I'm pregnant," she said. "And I need your help."

"Why would you need *my* help?" I asked. "Because that baby can't be mine."

Or could it? Had she already been pregnant when she left me?

No, that wasn't possible. Rick would have told me.

Or maybe not.

"No, of course not. It's Rick's," she said. "There's no doubt about that. He's the only one."

The only one. The words were like a knife in my gut and I had to force myself to relax my shoulders and breathe.

"What do you want from me?" I asked as I closed my eyes and rested my forehead on the doorjamb.

She paused. "I'm hoping you'll talk to Rick for me because he doesn't want me to have the baby."

I opened my eyes. "What do you mean, he doesn't want you to have it? Does he want you to have an abortion?"

"Yes."

The anger I felt initially—when I first heard her voice on the other end of the line—began to recede. It was replaced by something else. I'm not sure what exactly because I was distracted by logistics and a long list of questions.

"How far along are you?" I asked.

"About six weeks."

I sat down again. "Explain this to me, Angela. Do *you* want to have an abortion?"

"No. I want to have the baby. I tried talking to Rick but he won't budge. He says he's not ready for kids and he wants to get his career going first. You know...I think I would find it easier to go through with an abortion if I had a ring on my finger, but he's not ready for that either."

"You mean to say...you'd agree to have the abortion if he proposed to you?"

This made no sense to me, and I began to feel as if I might have dodged a bullet when Angela dumped me.

"Yes," she said, "because at least then I'd know there would be other children. But right now, I'm not sure about our future. He doesn't seem ready to commit."

I hate to say I told you so...

Leaning an elbow on the table, I cupped my forehead in a hand. "What do you want me to do about it, Angela?"

Did she actually think I would call Rick and try to talk him into marrying her?

"Could you talk to him for me?" she asked. "Could you get him to let me have this baby?"

I took my hand away from my face. "*Let* you have it?" Now I was angry. "It's not up to him," I said. "It's *your* body. He can't force you to have an abortion if you don't want to."

"But he said he wouldn't be happy if I had the baby. I'm afraid I might lose him if I don't do what he wants."

Oh, God. Was she really saying this?

"Then go ahead and lose him," I said. "If you want to have this baby, kick Rick to the curb because he won't be there for you either way. And he certainly doesn't deserve your devotion. I warned you when you left here that he wouldn't be there, not like I would have been. You know that I would have never forced you into..."

I stopped myself because we couldn't go back. Even if we could, I wouldn't want to. It was too late. But I didn't want to see Angela crushed by Rick's selfishness, either. I'd loved her once and nothing would ever change that.

I realized she was crying. Part of me wanted to comfort her, to take her into my arms and tell her everything was going to be okay, but I couldn't do that. We were on opposite sides of the country, and more importantly she was pregnant with my brother's child.

"I don't know what I'm going to do," she said. "I can't raise this baby alone and I'll die if he leaves me."

"You won't die," I told her. "You're a strong woman. You'll be just fine."

She continued to weep into the phone. "I want to have the baby. I really do."

"Then tell him that."

We sat in silence for a long time. I listened to her blow her nose.

At last she spoke. “Okay. I will.”

We chatted for a few more minutes until I sensed that she was feeling better.

Before we hung up, I asked her to keep me posted.

Because I couldn’t simply just forget about this.

Chapter Eighteen

The next night, at exactly the same time, my phone rang again. I quickly muted the television and dove across Bentley as he lay on the sofa beside me.

"Hello?"

"Hi, Jesse. It's me again. You said to keep you posted."

I recovered a more comfortable position. "Yeah. How did it go? What did he say?"

She took a deep breath and let it out. "I couldn't get him to change his mind about the baby but he told me to be patient. He said…maybe we could get engaged at Christmas. But he needs to focus on his career first so I want to give him that."

I frowned and sat forward on the edge of the sofa. "What are you saying? That you're going to have the abortion?"

"Yes," she replied. "He made an appointment for this Friday and Christmas isn't that far away. I can last until then and maybe next year we can try and have a baby, after he signs some clients of his own."

"Angela," I said, "he's not going to give you a ring this Christmas." I felt cruel speaking so bluntly but she needed to hear the truth.

"How do *you* know?"

"Because he's my brother and I know him."

"But you don't know *us*," she argued. "You don't know what we're like together."

I shut my eyes and shook my head. "I do remember what you said before you left—that it was intense."

"That's right."

"Is it *still* intense?" I asked. "Is it like it was when he came home for Christmas and you were sneaking around behind my back? Or has some of the excitement worn off?"

Angela fell silent. "That was different."

"Of course it was," I replied. "You were the forbidden fruit. Now you're not."

"Jesse!"

"I'm sorry," I said, "but I have to call a spade a spade, and the sooner you figure out what Rick's all about, the better off you'll be."

"No. You don't understand..."

I pinched the bridge of my nose and paused before I spoke.

"Maybe I don't," I replied with resignation.

"If you could only talk to him," she pleaded in a quivering voice. "Because I don't want to lose him."

Why was I having this conversation? Why was I getting involved?

"What about the baby?" I asked. "Do you want to lose him, or her?"

She hesitated, then answered firmly. "No, but Rick already made the appointment."

Ah, Christ. I was in it now. Deep. All the way up to my ears. I couldn't possibly walk away.

"What's your address?" I asked, reaching for a pen.

"Why?"

"Because I have the next three days off and I'm coming out there."

"Really?"

"Yes. So cancel the appointment for now, at least until we have a chance to talk about it. Will you do that?"

"Yes, I'll cancel it."

Meanwhile, I had no idea what I was doing or what I was going to say to Rick when I arrived. I had no plan, except to book a red-eye flight out that evening.

Chapter Nineteen

As luck would have it, my flight was delayed. A storm cell moved in and all the planes were grounded. Other incoming flights were rerouted and by midnight the airport had turned into a zoo full of angry animals. Passengers missed their connections and were stuck in the terminal all night. People shouted at the airline reps, who couldn't do much about the weather. As I witnessed the chaos, I was glad I was just a baggage handler.

Travelers had no choice but to sleep on the carpeted floors at the gates inside security while others crowded onto shuttles to the nearest hotels to wait out the storm.

Thankfully I was able to return home after I was rebooked on a flight for the following evening.

The storm passed and my boss managed to shift the schedule around. He told me to take a few extra days off so I wouldn't have to turn around and come right home as soon as I arrived in California.

"Have a great time," he said.

Sure. What a party it's going to be.

I boarded my flight that night and we took off without any further delays into a luminous sunset that took my breath away. It had been hell getting to that point, but suddenly I felt blessed to have been assigned a window seat where I could stare in awe at the pink horizon and the tiny white lights of the city below as we gained altitude.

When the sunlight faded to black and I could see nothing but darkness, I put on the headphones and watched a movie.

Then I fell asleep.

I woke after an hour or two, somewhere over the Midwest. The cabin lights flickered on and the pilot spoke to us through the noisy static of the speaker system.

He informed us that we would need to make an unscheduled landing in Salt Lake City because there might be some problems with the equipment. He was conspicuously vague about the nature of the problems and an immediate hush fell over the cabin interior.

Even the flight attendants appeared shaken and alarmed as they moved up and down the aisles, collecting empty plastic cups and crumpled up snack wrappers, while politely asking everyone to fasten their seatbelts and return their seats to the upright position.

The panicked sound of call buttons chiming overhead added to the tension, and the silence among the passengers was especially unnerving as we descended into the clouds and hit a bad patch of turbulence.

The woman in front of me threw up in her airsickness bag. The man beside me gripped the armrests so tightly his knuckles turned white.

Leaning back against the seat, he turned his head toward me. "I wonder what the problem is." His upper lip glistened with perspiration. His cheeks were pasty gray.

"I guess the pilot's too busy to explain," I replied as I turned to look at my reflection in the dark window.

Was this it? Was this how my life was going to end?

We continued to bump and jostle over tight air pockets in the clouds and I wondered if I was I going to die on this insane rescue mission to save my ex-girlfriend from making the worst mistake of her life.

And what would Bentley do if I never came home? Oh, Jesus, I'd put him in a kennel the day before. Would my parents go and collect him? I wanted to call them and ask if they would do that one last thing for me…

Really, God?

On top of everything else, is this really necessary? Can't you give me a break, just this once, when I'm trying to do something good for someone who stomped on my heart and crushed it like a bug?

In that precise instant, the turbulence came to a halt.

The rest of the descent was smooth and surprisingly ordinary, though it took some time for my raging pulse to decelerate to a normal rhythm.

We landed without any trouble in Salt Lake City, and as we touched down, the passengers broke into a spontaneous round of applause.

I never learned what went wrong with the equipment but we all discussed it tirelessly when we disembarked from the aircraft and had to wait in a long lineup to rebook on other flights.

I spent the rest of the night in the airport, sleeping on the floor at the departure gate, and woke up to learn that my next flight was going to be delayed as well. Evidently a few tornadoes in Oklahoma had thrown departure and arrival schedules into spinning vortexes all across the country.

Now it looked like I wouldn't land in LA until Friday morning.

I found a payphone and tried to call Angela.

Chapter Twenty

I called every hour and left messages until it was time to board my flight. By the time we landed at LAX, I felt like a giant bag of dirty laundry. Thankfully, I had packed all my belongings in a knapsack so at least I was able to brush my teeth and change my shirt before I got off the plane and climbed into a taxi.

It was my first time in Los Angeles but I was only minutely interested in the view outside the car window because I couldn't stop thinking about Angela. Maybe she thought I'd changed my mind about coming out here. I hoped my phone messages reached her.

But even if they had, I didn't know how I was going to solve her problems and make things better. Rick had never listened to me before when I tried to give him advice or when I asked him to do things. He always did whatever he damn well pleased. Whatever worked best for him.

Then what the bloody hell was I doing here? I wondered as we sped along the freeway. What did I hope to accomplish? Was I here simply to provide moral support for Angela? Or did I intend to be her knight in shining armor, as I had been that day in the parking lot when she locked her keys in the car?

I wasn't sure. All I knew was that I couldn't let Rick bully a person or manipulate her into doing something she didn't want to do.

Not this time.

~

There was no answer when I knocked on the door to Rick and Angela's apartment. This came as no surprise because I'd called ahead from the airport and was forced to leave another message on their answering machine.

I didn't have much money on me so I decided to hunker down in the corridor, rest my head on my knapsack and close my eyes until one of them returned home.

I slept for a long time. The trip across the country must have exhausted me more than I realized because when Rick kicked my foot—*hard*—for the umpteenth time, I startled awake, groggy and lightheaded. I squinted up at him in a daze.

"What are you doing here?" he asked with a frown.

He was dressed in a black suit with a blue tie and he carried a brown paper bag that looked and smelled like it might be full of Chinese food.

"What time is it?" I asked.

"Almost seven," he replied. "And you didn't answer my question. What the hell are you doing here? Did Angela call you?"

"Yeah." I rose stiffly to my feet.

He shook his head and dug into his pocket for the apartment keys. "I told her not to do that."

He unlocked the door and I followed him inside. While he set the bag of food on the table, I glanced around at the worn sofa, cluttered desk and metal bookshelf, and peered toward the kitchen, which was even smaller than mine.

"This is only temporary," Rick explained, "until I can afford a better place. I've only been working a couple of months."

"I'm not criticizing," I said. I glanced toward what I assumed was the bedroom door. "Angela's not here? Do you know where she is?"

"I haven't got a clue," Rick replied. "We had a huge fight last night so I left and slept on the couch at a friend's house." He shrugged out of his suit jacket, draped it on the back of a chair at the table and drew his tie out from under his crisp white shirt collar. He folded it on top of his jacket and began to rip open the paper bag containing his dinner.

"Now that I think about it," he added, "it's probably your fault we had the fight in the first place. And she didn't tell me you were coming."

"What did you fight about?" I asked, still standing by the door and finally sliding my backpack off my shoulder. I let it drop heavily to the floor.

Rick motioned me over. "Do you want some of this? There's plenty."

I hadn't eaten all day and the smell of the beef fried rice, chicken balls and egg rolls caused my mouth to water.

"Sure." I approached the table while Rick went to fetch plates and a couple of serving spoons.

"Chopsticks are in the bag," he said.

I helped him open the containers and we sat down to eat.

"So what did you and Angela fight about?" I asked a second time, growing concerned that she might have kept the appointment that morning after all.

His eyes lifted. "That's not really any of your business, is it?"

"I think it is," I replied, "since she used to be my girlfriend and she was pretty upset when she called me."

Rick picked up an egg roll, swirled it around the pool of plum sauce on his plate, and took a large bite. "I assume she told you then."

Losing my appetite all of a sudden, I sat back. "Yeah, she told me everything. Why else would I fly all the way out here?"

Rick pointed his chopsticks at me. "Then it *is* your fault. Because everything was going just fine until last night, when she told me she changed her mind about what we decided and that she'd cancelled the appointment."

I felt a great rush of relief to hear that she had stuck to her guns. I only wished I'd been there to back her up.

"So she didn't go through with it?" I asked.

"Not that I know of," he replied.

I wondered how he could have risen from bed that morning and gone to work all day, not knowing for sure. But that was Rick.

He scooped more rice out of the Styrofoam container and refilled his plate. "Let me guess," he said. "You offered to come out here and fix everything. You probably even told her you'd marry her."

"No," I said flatly. "That's not what I told her."

"But that's what you're hoping, isn't it? That you'll get her back?"

"No," I repeated more firmly. "I only came to help her figure out what she's going to do. She sounded like she needed a friend."

Rick rolled his eyes and scoffed. "Yeah, right. You keep telling yourself that."

"What is your *problem*?" I asked. "Why are you acting like I'm the selfish one here?"

"Selfish? Jesus! All I've done is give, give, give to that girl, but nothing's ever enough. Don't get me wrong, when she first came out here she was a lot of fun, but then she got all clingy and demanding, and all of a sudden, she wanted to get married. After five months! Honestly, I think she tried to trap me with this pregnancy. If it's even real. I have my doubts."

I had to pause a moment and consider what he was telling me, because I remembered how Angela had behaved when Rick flew home on New Year's Day. She didn't eat or speak to anyone. She hadn't seemed rational.

Certainly, through the years, Rick had sent more than a few girls into an emotional vortex of insanity, but maybe he wasn't always completely to blame for their highs and lows.

But had Angela truly been lying about the pregnancy? I didn't believe she would go that far…But what did I know? At the time, I hadn't even realized she was cheating on me with my own brother.

"Can I use your washroom?" I asked, because I needed to think this through. I needed to see Angela and talk to her face-to-face before I passed judgment.

"It's through there." Rick pointed toward the bedroom.

As I rose from my chair, I couldn't help but wonder what was going to happen when Angela walked through the door. Whether she was pregnant or not, I knew there was no chance Rick was ever going to marry her, but if he was leading her down that garden path it was time for him to set her straight. She needed to know the truth so that she could get on with her life.

As I moved through the bedroom, I glanced briefly at the unmade bed and felt a sudden, sharp pang of jealousy.

It was enough to stop me in my tracks. The image of Rick sleeping with Angela was more than I could stomach. I had to shut my eyes and fight hard to purge the thought from my brain.

Then I began to question my feelings.

Was I truly over her? What if she decided to leave Rick and come home, pregnant and alone? Could I forgive her for any of this?

God, oh God…

I opened my eyes again and put one foot in front of the other. Maybe this jealousy had nothing to do with Angela and was merely a product of my resentment toward Rick. Those roots were certainly buried deep. The seeds had been planted many years ago—on the day he drove me home from a football game and refused to hit the brakes when I asked him to.

As I pushed the bathroom door open, however, all thoughts of the past flew out of my head, for there was Angela, lying on the white tile floor in a puddle of blood.

Adrenaline spiked through my body and I rushed to her side. "Rick!" I shouted. "Get in here! And call 911!"

Chapter Twenty-one

We learned, after the paramedics arrived, that Angela had not tried to commit suicide but had most likely attempted to perform an abortion on herself by using the knitting needle they found on the floor beside her.

Later, the autopsy would show that she had indeed been pregnant, so there could be no doubt about whether or not she had lied to Rick about her condition in order to trap him. She'd been telling the truth about that—and the fact that I had not arrived in time to help her would haunt me for the rest of my days.

In that moment however, after they wheeled Angela into the ambulance and Rick and I were left alone, there were other issues to discuss.

"What did you say to her last night?" I asked, feeling distraught and needing answers as I followed him back into his apartment.

Rick went straight to the kitchen and pulled a cold beer out of the fridge. He twisted off the cap, pitched it into the trash can and tipped the bottle up. Then he leaned back against the counter and faced me. "Do you want one?"

"No!" I replied, leaning a shoulder against the doorjamb between the kitchen and living room. "I just want to know what happened. Tell me what you said to her and why you left her alone."

"I wasn't her babysitter," he replied. "And I didn't say anything."

"You must have. You said you had a fight. She couldn't have been arguing with herself."

Rick set his beer down on the counter. "Fine. If you really want to know, she told me she cancelled the appointment for this morning because she wanted to think about it some more. She wanted me to think about it, too, but I told her I'd already made up my mind and I wasn't going to change it. I told her I didn't want to have a kid or get married. Not today. Not ever. I was honest with her, Jesse."

I felt my eyebrows pull together in a frown. "How did she take it?"

"How do you *think* she took it? You know how emotional she was. She cried and begged and pleaded."

Suddenly there was a heavy pounding in my ears and a heated blood flow to all my extremities. My fingers began to twitch and before I knew what I was doing, I had stalked across the kitchen and grabbed hold of Rick's shirt in my fists.

"What is wrong with you?" I demanded to know. "She's *dead!* Don't you care?"

I was no longer the nerdy baby brother who couldn't fight back when he was surrounded by linebackers. I was now as tall as he was and I'd been chucking heavy suitcases for a year. Tonight it was just the two of us, alone in his small kitchen.

He tried to slap my hands away but my grip was rock solid as I dragged him along the length of the counter and shoved him up against the refrigerator.

"Of course I care," he replied.

"No, you don't. You never loved her. Not like I did. She was nothing to you."

"She was something," he said, "but you need to calm down, Jesse, because she wasn't *that* special. Remember, she cheated on you."

I dragged him away from the fridge and shoved him so hard up against the wall, I knocked the breath out of him. "Don't you ever say that again."

Suddenly he head-butted me in the nose and pain shot through my skull. I saw stars and stumbled back a few steps. The next thing I knew Rick was hauling me into the living room by the shirt collar and throwing me onto the sofa.

"Get a grip!" he shouted, standing over me and pointing a finger. "You're upset."

"Damn right, I'm upset." I wiped at my nose with the back of my hand and realized I was bleeding. "Jesus."

He pointed at me again. "Stay down." I thought maybe his intention was to fetch me a washcloth or something to staunch the flow of blood, but he made no move to administer first aid. He simply stood there, staring at me with a look of warning.

"If you grab me again," he said, "I swear I'll finish you."

That was all I could take. Something exploded in me and the whole world turned red. I shot like a rocket off the sofa and tackled him onto his back on the living room floor.

I punched him in the face but he punched me back which caused a ringing in my ears.

Grabbing him by the shirt, I hauled him to his feet and threw him into a small table. The lamp smashed to the floor.

Rick scrambled to his feet and launched himself back at me. He pummeled me in the stomach, then his fist connected with my jaw. Dizziness swirled around in my brain. I couldn't seem to comprehend how to curl my hands into fists in order to fight back. My brain was in a fog. He hit me again and again.

The beating eventually stopped, but it took me a few seconds to realize that Rick was now on the other side of the room. How had he gotten over there? My cheekbones were throbbing, my lip was split open and bleeding, but I couldn't feel much pain anywhere else. Everything was numb.

I squinted at my brother and wasn't sure how, or when, I had caused so much damage, because there was blood pouring out of his nose and he was doubled over, clutching a rib.

"Get out of here," he said. "Go home and don't ever come back here."

I bent to pick up my backpack on the floor. "Don't worry, I won't," I said, "because I don't ever want to see your face again."

Two days later, I was staring out another airplane window as we lifted off the runway at sunset.

I had called Angela's parents immediately after walking out of Rick's apartment. Obviously they were devastated and inconsolable but grateful for my phone call. After a lengthy conversation, they entrusted me with the grim duty of bringing Angela's remains home to be buried in their family plot.

It was the worst week of my life.

I wondered what my parents were going to say about all of it.

A New Life

Chapter Twenty-two

Nadia Carmichael

It was the dream that woke me.

Again.

I was keeping count now, and this was the fourth time in the past two weeks.

Something was different tonight, however. As my eyes fluttered open in the darkness, I was able to remember the striking and vivid images of what I'd seen below me in the dream—and this time I did not wake in a panic, fearing for my life.

Allow me to explain. My name is Nadia Carmichael and almost a year ago, I contracted a virus that attacked my heart muscle. My health deteriorated quickly until I wound up in the ICU suffering from heart failure.

To complicate things more, I was six months pregnant at the time and completely alone because the father of my child wanted nothing to do with me. He paid me a generous lump sum to disappear from his life forever, release him of all obligations and promise never to ask him for anything more.

Thankfully my twin sister Diana took me in when I was ill and waiting for the transplant. She has since helped me care for my baby daughter, Ellen, who was born healthy last fall and is the light of both our lives.

But it has not been an easy road to get here. Since the transplant eight months ago, I have lived in an almost constant state of anxiety while my body adjusted to my new heart.

Although, perhaps "adjusted" is too simple a word, because twice now, follow-up cardiac biopsies revealed that my immune system was rejecting the unfamiliar organ inside me. My body had viewed my new heart as a foreign invader and had attempted to fight it off.

This is actually quite a common occurrence for organ transplant recipients. To combat this, I take immunosuppressive drugs, which I will take for the rest of my life. The downside is that they weaken my immune system overall and put me at greater risk for all sorts of other infections.

For this reason I was forced to live like a hermit the first few months after my transplant and avoid public places where germs were prevalent. I had to wear a mask when I went out, but thankfully my pathology reports have shown significant improvement lately and I no longer have to wear the mask.

Oddly, it was when I began to feel better and was able to resume a more normal lifestyle that the flying dreams began.

Sometimes I fly like a bird, low over water, but most of the time I soar over cities at night. I'm not sure why it's always nighttime in my dreams. Perhaps I enjoy all the lights in the tall buildings and on the freeways below. The red taillights on a long stretch of road are especially mesmerizing. So is the starlight when I look up, though the stars are not always visible. Sometimes I fly just under a blanket of clouds—or maybe it's smog; I'm never sure.

Have you ever dreamed you were flying? If so, were you speeding along like a bullet through tunnels, or coasting over fields and mountains like a bird?

Chapter Twenty-three

Ellen woke me at sunrise the next morning. Wishing it wasn't time to get up yet, I rolled over to watch her in her crib. We shared a room together in my sister's house in Beacon Hill. Diana, my identical twin, was a successful divorce lawyer and she occupied the room at the end of the hall, though sometimes she slept over at her fiancé's house.

Incidentally, that was something good that came from my illness, because that's how Diana met Jacob. He was the cardiac surgeon in charge of my case. Coincidentally, he lived in our neighborhood as well, so he was always nearby, handy in an emergency.

There had been more than a few of those over the past year.

A knock sounded at my door and I leaned up on an elbow. "Come in."

"Want me to take her?" Diana asked, peeking her head into my room. "I'm up anyway."

"It's Saturday," I replied. "You should be sleeping in."

"So should you." She padded across my room in her bathrobe and slippers. Approaching the crib, she began to speak in a melodic voice. "Good morning, little angel." She reached into the crib and gathered Ellen into her arms. "Are you hungry? How about we change your diaper first?"

I lay my head back down on the pillow and watched my sister carry my baby girl to the change table. Diana was cooing and smiling and I couldn't help but appreciate the fact that despite my suffering over the past year, and the hardships that still lay ahead, there was so much to be grateful for.

"I had the dream again," I mentioned to Diana as I rolled onto my back.

She removed Ellen's diaper and reached for a fresh unscented baby wipe. "That's the second time this week."

"Fourth time this month," I added, "but last night's dream was different."

Diana glanced at me with interest. "In what way?" She lifted Ellen's behind off the table to slide the clean diaper into place, then fastened all the Velcro tabs.

"I recognized where I was," I said, "and I'm a little freaked out about it."

"Why?" she asked as she picked Ellen up again.

"Because I was flying away from the transplant center," I replied. "It was all very clear and familiar. I flew over Cambridge Street, the grassy Common and Chinatown. It was the first time I recognized any place in one of these dreams. Before that, I just thought I was flying over imaginary locations—random fields and rivers, towns I had never been to."

"What do you think it means?" Diana asked, bobbing at the knees to entertain Ellen.

Feeling restless, I sat up, tossed the covers aside and swung my feet to the floor. "I feel foolish saying it."

"Don't feel foolish." She moved to stand before me. "Tell me."

Curling my fingers around the edge of the mattress, I looked up at my sister with bewilderment. "Do you think it's possible that these dreams are somehow connected to my donor? Do you think he's flying in here to check on me or something?" Then I shook my head. "It sounds crazy, doesn't it? Maybe I need a brain transplant."

Diana sat down beside me and I reached to take Ellen from her.

"You're not crazy," Diana said. "When you got sick, I did a lot of research. I read that many people have reported similar experiences. They sometimes feel differently afterwards, their tastes change and they feel some connection to the donor."

"But isn't that just psychological?" I asked. "There's no scientific proof to support that, surely. Most doctors say that the heart is just a pump."

"Doctors and scientists don't know everything," she replied. "Organ transplantation is still fairly new. You know, I read about a guy who always hated onions. Then he had a heart transplant and suddenly he couldn't get enough of them. He met the donor's family and found out that his donor loved onions. It was his favorite food—raw, sautéed, fried..."

I cradled Ellen in my arms and smiled down at her. "Do you hear that? A man hated onions and then he loved them. How weird is that?" I turned my attention back to my sister. "I wish I knew more about my donor."

Unfortunately, there were strict rules of confidentiality in place to guard everyone's privacy. All I had been told was age and gender. He was male and twenty-eight—the same age as me—when he died. I didn't know the cause of death, but I couldn't shake the feeling that it had been some sort of accident.

I'd written a letter of thanks to the family (which we are permitted to do as long as we don't reveal our identity). The organ donor network took care of delivering it for me. According to protocol, if the donor's family ever wished to make contact, it could be arranged as long as we were both willing and eager.

I hadn't heard back from the family—at least not yet—and I could only presume they would find it too painful to meet me, or that they simply wanted to move on with their lives.

I often thought about how they must still be grieving for their lost loved one—and though I was immensely grateful for the generous gift that saved my life, there were also feelings of guilt.

Why was I the lucky one? Why had I survived and not him? Was it somehow fated that he would live and die so that I could have his heart when I needed it?

Diana pushed a lock of my hair behind my ear. "Maybe you should talk to somebody about this."

"Like who?" I asked. "A shrink?"

She considered that for a moment. "No. I mean somebody who might be more open-minded about this sort of thing. When I was researching everything to do with organ transplantation, I came across a book written by a woman who lives somewhere here in New England. She had an out-of-body, near-death experience a few years ago and sometimes she speaks in public about the possibility of life after death. I saw something in the paper the other day, which is why I'm mentioning it. I think she's going to be in town doing a book signing. You should go. I'll watch Ellen for you."

"A near-death experience?" I asked. "That seems way out there."

She gave me a look. "You have someone else's heart beating inside of you. If that's not way out there, I don't know what is."

Ellen started to fuss, so we took her downstairs to feed her.

Chapter Twenty-four

As it turned out, the woman who had written the book about her near-death experience came to town the following week to do a reading at an independent bookstore that specialized in non-fiction and self-help books.

I decided to follow Diana's advice and check it out, but first I ordered her book online and downloaded it to my tablet. The woman's name was Sophie Duncan and she told the story of how her car skidded off a country road on a winter night and rolled over onto a frozen lake. The ice broke and her vehicle sank to the bottom. By the time the rescue team pulled her out, she'd been dead for at least twenty minutes but the freezing temperature of the water slowed her body systems down, and they were able to revive her.

The book described how she watched from above as the paramedics warmed her up in the ambulance. Later she witnessed the medical team shock her back to life in the ER.

As I read the book, I couldn't help but wonder if my donor had had a similar out-of-body experience when he died. Had he watched from above as the doctors removed the working heart from his body and placed it into mine?

It all seemed very far-fetched, and Sophie's story read more like a novel. Surely it had to be fiction. But when I found myself standing in the bookstore in front of her table, looking down at her as she smiled up at me, I knew she wasn't some New Age quack. There was an intelligence about her. She seemed grounded.

"Hi there," she said, reaching for one of the books on the table and opening it to the title page. With her pen poised and ready, she said, "What's your name? Would you like me to make it out to you?"

I felt rather awestruck because she was a bestselling author, yet at the same time I felt I knew her, that we shared a personal connection. Though I supposed everyone who read her book felt that way, because she had shared something very personal and intimate with all of us.

"That would be great," I said. "My name's Nadia."

While she squiggled a few words and signed her name, I said, "I already read it as an eBook because I was interested in what happened to you. I've been having some strange out-of-body experiences myself."

She closed the book and looked up at me. "Really?"

Nervously, I continued. "Yes. I had a heart transplant eight months ago and I keep having these recurring dreams that I'm flying. Sometimes I'm flying over the hospital where the transplant surgery was performed."

She tilted her head to the side. "That's interesting. I've never spoken to an organ transplant recipient before. Lots of NDEs, but your story's a bit different."

I nodded. "I'm not really sure what to make of it. I don't know if I'm just dreaming, or if it's a memory of what I did and where I went while I was on the table. Or maybe…" I paused.

"Maybe what?" she asked, leaning forward slightly.

I felt silly suggesting it, which was silly in itself because the person I was speaking to claimed publicly to have traveled to heaven and back. She even wrote a book about it.

“Tell me,” she said, handing the autographed book to me.

I hugged it to my chest and spoke quietly. “I wonder if it’s the person whose heart I have inside of me. Maybe it’s his soul flying around and we’re connected somehow. Or maybe he had some unfinished business and he can’t leave to go wherever it is we’re supposed to go after we die.”

Sophie stared at me for a long moment, then reached down to pick up her purse. She dug into it for a small notepad and jotted something down.

“This is a book you should read,” she said. “It’s about cellular memory and there are some references to organ transplants. I met the author at a convention once. He’s a smart guy and has done a ton of research. He has a website so you can contact him if you want to. He might be able to answer some of your questions, but more likely, he’ll want to pick *your* brain. You should also look into astral projection. That’s something different, but maybe in your case it’s some sort of combination of the two.”

She handed me the piece of paper and I realized I was holding up the line. There was still a large crowd of readers and fans behind me.

“Thank you,” I said. “This has been really helpful.” Mostly, I was grateful to talk to someone who didn’t think I was completely delusional.

“Good luck,” she replied, “and congratulations on getting that new heart.”

I smiled at her. “I appreciate that. I feel very blessed.”

Over the next few days, in between Ellen’s bottle feedings and walks to the park with the stroller, I researched the subject of cellular memory and read a few memoirs written by people who had undergone organ transplants.

I also investigated astral projection, which is another form of out-of-body experience, but does not always accompany death. It can happen during sleep or other altered states like meditation or surgeries. There were even some websites that provided instructions on how to do it and control it.

While I learned a great deal about different alternative theories—and took the skepticism into consideration as well—none of it answered the burning question in my mind about what my dreams truly meant. I had nothing tangible to offer as evidence of a spiritual or cellular connection to my donor because I had no idea who he was, where he'd lived, or whether or not he liked onions…or anything else.

Nor was I making an effort to take my spirit on a joy ride each night. It was beyond my control, and in all honesty, it just felt like I was dreaming.

I suppose that made me as much of a skeptic as the next person.

Chapter Twenty-five

Two weeks went by, and because I stayed up late reading each night, I slept like a log. There were no thrilling expeditions out the window and over treetops and telephone poles. There were no dazzling aerial views of the city at night.

Eventually I began to let go of the desire to know more about the man whose heart now beat inside my chest. I was too busy with motherhood and the requirements of my recovery to dwell on much else outside my daily routines. I was focused on Ellen's laughter in the park, the way she slept soundly in her crib and the miracle of her first baby steps.

She was only eleven months old when she walked from Diana's arms to mine in the kitchen one evening. A prodigy, surely. A future gymnast or perhaps a long distance runner. I suppose dreams come in many forms.

Nevertheless, the memories of my nighttime escapades were ever-present in my mind, hovering there like curious hummingbirds. Each night when I slipped into bed I gazed out the window and wondered if I would go flying.

Each morning I woke up feeling disappointed.

Then the letter arrived.

"It can't be possible," I said to Diana when I finished reading it. "Full custody...Can he even do this? Why would he want to? There's got to be something else going on here because you know what he's like. He can't actually want to be a father to Ellen."

Diana read the letter a second time, then set it down on the table. "As a parent, he does have legal rights. I just never thought he—of all people—would want to exercise them."

It was a long and complicated story, but Diana knew my baby's father, Rick, better than most people because she'd almost married him two years ago. I saved her from that certain peril, however, when I fell for his charms myself and was the cause of their breakup. Less than a year later, I was alone and pregnant with Rick's child, waiting for a heart transplant.

Now this.

"Didn't he say good-bye to those rights," I asked, "when he told me he wanted no part in Ellen's upbringing and paid me to stay away? I signed a legal document promising not to ask him for child support or anything else if I accepted the money."

"That protected him, not you," Diana said. "The Family Code is written to assure that children have frequent and continued contact with both parents after they separate, and it encourages parents to share rights and responsibilities. So if he's asking for full custody, he must have something up his sleeve."

"But what if it's not in the child's best interests?" I asked. "Rick doesn't even know Ellen. He's never seen her or held her. He doesn't know her sleep schedule or what she likes to eat."

I felt sick to my stomach at the thought that I could lose any of my rights as a mother. That my child would be separated from all that was familiar and full of love. Her life would be drastically changed. I couldn't bear to think of handing Ellen over to a man who thought only of himself. Rick had never wanted a child. He didn't love her.

"When it comes to proving what's best for the child," Diana explained, "you'd have to show that Rick would be an unfit parent and I can tell you right now that would be virtually impossible. Rick is charming, successful, wealthy, law-abiding and brilliant. He could sell snow to Santa Clause. I just don't understand why he's asking for full custody or how he thinks he can get it. It surprises me."

I rested my elbows on the table and bowed my head. "Doesn't he know I named *you* as Ellen's legal guardian in my will? You're the best person to take over because she knows you and loves you. And you've supported us both through all the hard times recently. Was Rick there? No. Did he offer any help? Of course not."

"He does know I'm named as her guardian in the will," Diana explained. "The last time I spoke to him, he seemed relieved to hear it. But obviously, he's changed his mind."

"But *why*?" I asked. "This isn't like him at all. Something must have happened, because the last time I checked his Facebook page, he was enjoying the single life quite a bit."

Diana raised an eyebrow. "How long ago was that?"

I rolled my eyes. "It was a long time ago. And you can be darn sure that I haven't given that jerk a single thought since the day I took all his money."

"You didn't take *all* his money," Diana reminded me. "He has plenty left over to hire a hot shot lawyer, so we need to take this seriously. We need to decide what we're going to do."

The baby monitor lights flickered and Ellen began to cry.

"I'll get her," I said, rising to my feet, "because I don't want to waste a single moment with her."

As I climbed the stairs to our room, I thought about Rick living on the other side of the country. How, exactly, did he expect to work out any sort of custody arrangement? Did he really think I would put Ellen on a plane and wave good-bye forever?

No. That was not going to happen.

I'd fight him to the death if I had to.

Chapter
Twenty-six

That night, shortly after I fell asleep, the dream came to me again. It had been more than two weeks since I'd gone flying and after the dream, when I woke and sat up in the darkness, I felt surprisingly calm.

Was this dream some sort of defense mechanism? I wondered. Was it my body's way of escaping the stress in my life? A way to protect my new heart?

When I rose the next morning, the day was hazy and humid. I changed Ellen's diaper, then tiptoed to Diana's room to see if she was awake yet. Her bed had not been slept in which was not unusual since she became engaged to Jacob.

I carried Ellen downstairs to the kitchen and warmed up a bottle, then settled myself comfortably on the sofa to watch an early morning re-run of Gilligan's Island.

After Ellen gulped down the entire contents of her bottle I shifted her in my arms, held her over my shoulder and patted her on the back. She let out an unladylike burp.

"Wow. *That* was something," I said in her ear. "But hey, I'm not judging."

The Gilligan's Island end credits played and Ellen fell back to sleep. I carried her to the kitchen and gently laid her down in the carrier, then plugged in the kettle to make a cup of tea while I cooked some oatmeal.

As my breakfast boiled on the stove I re-read the letter from Rick's lawyer and tried to figure out how I was going to deal with this mountain in front of me.

"My client wishes to know his daughter and wants to establish a parental relationship as soon as possible."

That was the part that stumped me. The wording made it sound almost urgent—as if Rick couldn't bear to be away from his daughter for another minute of his life.

I supposed that was how these divorce lawyers operated. They charged ahead aggressively. It could have nothing to do with Rick's true wants or desires. The lawyer just wanted to win.

Feeling a sudden stroke of genius, I stood up from the table and padded into the den to turn on the computer. As far as I knew, Rick and I were still Facebook friends and I was curious about what was going on in his life recently. Was he in a relationship? Maybe his new girlfriend wanted a cute baby to cuddle and he wanted to get one for her.

When I logged on and searched for Rick, however, I discovered that he had deleted his Facebook account which seemed odd, considering he represented athletes and sports celebrities and was in the business of networking with people.

I could just call him, I thought, but wanted to check with Diana first, because I didn't want to jeopardize my position. My relationship with Rick hadn't exactly been mature. I had lost my temper with him more than once and I didn't want to give him any new ammunition to use against me in court.

If it even came to that.

I hoped it wouldn't, because I wasn't sure my new heart could weather that much stress.

Chapter Twenty-seven

"I was thinking," Diana said to me that night after I settled Ellen in her crib, "that the gloves need to come off and we need to fight hard and convince the court that Rick is not a fit parent for Ellen. It's unlikely we can prevent him from seeing her if he wants to, but we can at least try to keep any custody rights to a minimum and keep me listed as her legal guardian in the event of your death."

"How would we do that?"

"By focusing on his single lifestyle and the parade of women who come and go from his condo. But even with that, I still think a judge will rule in his favor—at least with partial custody—because he *is* the father."

"What if he's with someone?" I asked. "Engaged or something. That plan could totally backfire if he's in a stable relationship and I'm...Well, nothing about my life has been stable since I got sick. I'm also a single mother. We have to find out his status."

I sat down on the sofa and Diana joined me.

"I checked for Rick's Facebook page this morning," I told her, "but he took it down so there's no way of knowing if he's still single."

"I noticed that." Diana rested her head on her hand. "And his phone number was disconnected. I tried calling directory assistance but there was no number listed for him in LA. I also called the agency but they said he was on vacation. He may very well have moved in with someone for all we know."

"It's strange, don't you think," I said, "that he's suddenly so inaccessible?"

"Yes," Diana replied, "and we need to know what's going on with him before we formulate a plan. Who knows, maybe he really has turned over a new leaf and wants to be a good dad. Maybe it *would* be in Ellen's best interests to invite him back into your life. If nothing else, he could offer financial support."

I scoffed. "Call me jaded, but I can't imagine how he would be good for Ellen in any way. He broke your heart, then he broke mine and countless others, no doubt. I don't want him to break Ellen's heart as soon as he starts to feel boxed in, because that seems to be a pattern with him."

"Believe me, I know," Diana said. "But he's Ellen's biological father and you might not have any choice in the matter."

I stood and walked to the window, stared out at the darkness. "It feels as if all my life I've been fighting one battle after another. Nothing's ever easy, is it?"

"Life should come with a warning label," Diana replied. "Caution. Ups and downs ahead. Proceed with extreme care."

A thought came to me suddenly, and I swung around to face Diana. "Did Rick ever mention his brother to you?"

Her eyebrows lifted. "No. *Rick has a brother?* I lived with him for over a year and he never told me that. He said he was an only child."

"The brother's name is Jesse," I told her. "And he probably didn't mention it to you because he wasn't proud of the fact that they haven't spoken to each other in over ten years. Rick never told me why but I'm pretty sure there's some dark and dirty skeleton in the closet between the two of them. Rick said he thought Jesse lived here on the east coast but he wasn't sure."

Diana stood. "Rick grew up in Connecticut. I know that much, and his parents still live here. His father's a dentist. I met them once when they came to LA to visit. They never mentioned another son."

I inclined my head. "If Rick and Jesse are estranged, do you think Jesse might be willing to tell us why? Maybe he has some information that would be helpful."

Diana blinked a few times. She was probably still in shock that Rick had a brother she never knew about. "It depends on what happened between them and what kind of person Jesse is. If he's a drug addict or in prison or something, he wouldn't be credible."

"How can we find out?" I asked. "Do you know Rick's parents well enough to contact them?"

"Oh no," she replied. "I wouldn't go that route. They're probably gung ho to help Rick get custody of their only grandchild. Besides that, if they didn't disclose to me that they had another son when I met them, they're probably estranged from Jesse, too. Ashamed of him most likely."

We stared at each other intensely.

"Let's go look him up online," I suggested.

Diana nodded. "Great minds think alike."

We both made a beeline to the computer in the den.

Chapter Twenty-eight

There were dozens of Jesse Frasers on Facebook. Though we were able to narrow the results down slightly, based on approximate age and location, it was impossible to locate the man we were searching for. We didn't even know if Jesse was older or younger than Rick.

Eventually we gave up and shuffled off to bed. I had trouble falling asleep, however, because something very powerful was compelling me to find this man. I felt certain that he would help us somehow and that my future with Ellen depended on our finding him.

When I woke the next morning after a restless and dreamless sleep, I fed Ellen in the kitchen and waited for Diana to come downstairs before she headed off to work.

"Good morning," she said as she entered the kitchen in a black skirt, blazer and heels. "Good, you made coffee." She poured herself a cup and kissed Ellen on the top of the head.

"I figured you could use it. We were up late last night. Did you sleep okay? Because I hardly slept a wink. I couldn't stop thinking about Rick's brother. I really want to find him and talk to him. I just have a funny feeling."

Diana sipped her coffee. "Then we should keep looking because if there's one thing I've learned in life, it's never to ignore a gut feeling." She reached for a banana in the fruit bowl and peeled it. "I know a guy who might be able to help. The firm uses him sometimes to dig up information. If I tell him the names of Rick's parents, he'll probably be able to get us a phone number and address fairly quickly."

"That would be great. Would you do that?"

"Yeah, no problem," she replied. "Now I have to run. Enjoy your exercise today, but don't overdo it."

She grabbed her briefcase from the hall and walked out the front door. Suddenly the house seemed quiet until Ellen started beating her spoon on the tray of her high chair.

With the sun shining in the kitchen window, I sat down at the table to organize my medications. I lined up all my pills in a row and took them, one by one with my oatmeal and a glass of orange juice.

Later I slathered myself and Ellen with sunscreen, buckled her into the stroller, and we went for our daily walk. It had taken many months to work up to this level of fitness after my surgery, but now, each morning, we walked briskly for one hour.

On that particular morning, despite my lack of sleep, I felt remarkably energetic.

Oh, how I loved my new heart.

By the time we arrived home again, Ellen was asleep in the stroller. I picked up the mail and had time to flip through the envelopes on the front step before unlocking the door.

One letter caught my eye, however.

Quickly I sat down on the step and ripped it open right there, because the envelope had come from the organ donor network.

I immediately began to read…

Chapter Twenty-nine

To the recipient of my son's heart,

Thank you for your letter. It meant a great deal to us to learn that something good came from my son's passing—that you are alive now because of the choice he made to donate his organs. We have heard from some others as well, so it appears his generosity has helped more than a few people.

Thank you again for telling us about your improved health. We were pleased and uplifted to hear it.

We wish you all the best.

Sincerely,

The Donor Family

I'm not sure what I had expected, but as I sat there in the bright sunshine on Diana's front step, a crushing wave of disappointment washed over me. It seemed such a brief and impersonal reply, like a form letter that they probably sent out to all the organ recipients who contacted them.

What had I hoped for, exactly? To meet the family? To see a picture of my donor? To learn what sort of life he had led?

Was he married? Educated? Was he a loner? How did he die?

Clearly, however, this family did not want to meet me, otherwise they would have shared more. The tone of the letter definitely implied that they preferred to end any future correspondence here.

A tear slid down my cheek and I wasn't sure why I was crying. Was it the fact that I'd just lost all hope of learning more about my donor? Or was it because I shared this family's grief? I never knew this woman's son but he had given me his heart and today it was beating inside my chest, keeping me alive so that I could know and raise my daughter. My donor's generosity had affected me in a profound and extraordinary way. I wanted so badly to thank him. But I couldn't.

And what about the dreams? Would I ever know what they meant or why I was having them night after night?

As I rose to my feet I wondered what would happen if I wrote another letter to the family and told them about my dreams, because I simply couldn't fathom the idea of giving up. I felt certain that these dreams represented something important.

"I think we found him," Diana said that evening when she walked through the front door.

"Who?" I asked, thinking of my donor of course, because he had been at the front of my mind all day.

"Rick's brother." Diana set her purse down on the table in the front hall and entered the kitchen where Ellen sat in her high chair waiting for the next spoonful.

"And good news," Diana added. "He's not a prison convict or a drug addict."

"Wonderful!" I spooned some pureed carrots into Ellen's mouth. She made a funny face. "Do you know where he lives?" I asked. "Can we contact him?"

"We can try. I'm not sure if he'll want to help us, though."

"Why not?"

Diana gave Ellen a kiss on the head and sat down. "Would *you* want to get involved in a child custody battle concerning two strangers you'd never met and a brother you hadn't spoken to in over ten years?"

"No," I replied honestly. "But maybe he has an axe to grind."

"Wouldn't that be terrific," Diana said, her tone dripping with sarcasm.

"So what do we do now?" I scraped the plastic baby spoon around the bottom of the carrot bowl and gave the last bit to Ellen.

Diana leaned close to her and spoke in baby talk. "We call him!" Ellen smiled and laughed. "Or rather, your lawyer will call," Diana added.

"You know I can't afford a lawyer," I reminded her. "I have no money."

Diana stood up. "Which is why it's a good thing my specialty is family law and I have a lot of friends. I have someone in mind for this and he's excellent. His name is Bob. I'll take care of this, so don't worry about it."

I smiled up at her. "What would I do without you?"

"I have no idea." She went to get some ice water from the refrigerator dispenser.

"When will you call?" I asked.

Ice cubes clattered into her tumbler and she checked her watch. "Look at that. It's supper hour. Now's as good a time as any. I'll make the call from my room."

With that, she finished filling her glass, carried it to the stairs and picked up her briefcase.

I had been waiting all day to tell her about the letter I'd received from the organ donor network, but I decided it could wait.

Chapter Thirty

Ten minutes later Diana descended the stairs. "You're seriously not going to believe this…"

I finished wiping the plastic tray on Ellen's high chair, then picked up the toy key ring she'd just dropped on the floor and handed it back to her. "What happened?"

Diana entered the kitchen. "I called the number we found for him today, which was for an area code in New Hampshire, but it said that number had been disconnected."

"Great," I replied. "So we're back to square one?"

"No, they gave me a new number—for an address right here in Boston."

I stopped what I was doing and faced her. "You're kidding me. Did you call it? Did you talk to him?"

"I did but there was no answer. I heard his voice on the answering machine though."

"Did you leave a number for him to call you back?"

"Yes," she replied. "I didn't tell him what it was about, though. I didn't want to scare him off. I just told him it concerned his brother and it was urgent."

"So now we just wait?" I asked.

Diana nodded and Ellen pitched the toy key ring onto the floor again. I picked it up, wiped it off, and handed it back to her.

"Since we have time," I said, "I want to tell you about the letter that came for me today. Have a seat and I'll get you a bowl of stew."

Diana sat down at the table, but before I served up the stew, I went to fetch the letter out of my purse. I wanted her to read it herself.

~

After she read the letter, Diana replied tactfully, "Well…it's nice that they responded."

I set a bowl of stew in front of her. "I've been telling myself that all day but I'm still disappointed. I really wanted to know more about my donor. I was hoping I might even get to meet the family, maybe see a picture of him."

Diana set the letter down. "It sounds like they don't want that."

"I know and I have to respect their privacy. What I need to do is move on and let it go. Whoever he is, he's gone now and I'm sure it's silly for me to imagine that his spirit is flying in and out of my bedroom at night to visit his old heart."

Diana dipped her spoon into the broth. "I'm sorry. I'm sure it's not easy."

"No, especially when I've been doing so much reading on cellular memory. I was even thinking about contacting that guy who wrote the book about it—the one Sophie Duncan mentioned. But what's the point if I don't know anything about my donor?"

"I'm sure it will all become clear eventually," Diana said. "Sometimes things happen for a reason and maybe you're just not meant to meet that family right now."

"But why *not* now?" I pressed. "Do you think I'm not ready for it? And does this mean I should give up? Because I was considering writing another letter to the family to tell them about my flying dreams. Who knows, maybe they're having the same ones."

My sister made a face. "I don't know if that would be a good idea. If they're not into that stuff they might think you're a nutcase."

"But I *am* a nut," I replied with a smile. "Always will be."

Just then the telephone rang and Diana immediately shoved her chair back to stand up. "I'll get it. It might be him."

By "him," she meant Rick's brother, while I couldn't stop thinking of someone else.

Chapter Thirty-one

Diana picked up the phone in the kitchen. "Hello, Diana Moore speaking."

Her gaze shot to mine and she nodded to let me know it was *him*. Rick's brother. My stomach did a somersault.

"Thanks for returning my call." Diana walked into the living room and sat down on the sofa.

I remained with Ellen so as not to be a distraction—though I strained to listen in as best I could.

Diana explained the situation to Mr. Fraser.

There was a long pause. Then she spoke again. "Yes, that's right. Yes. Uh huh. That would be great."

Ellen suddenly became chatty and started wiggling in her chair. I moved to unbuckle her and set her free for a while so she could toddle around the table.

I heard Diana rise from the sofa. She returned to the kitchen.

By this time, my heart was racing and I could barely contain my curiosity. "Was it him?" I asked. "What did he say?"

Diana set the cordless phone in the charger and returned to finish her stew. "It was him all right and he was very surprised to hear what I was calling about."

"Did he offer to help us?" I asked.

She hesitated. "Not exactly, but I still want to talk to him some more. He seemed uneasy and a bit reluctant, but I managed to convince him to meet us."

I stared at her in shock. "Really?"

"Yes. I thought about inviting him over here, but I don't want to give him our home address because we don't know anything about him." She picked up her spoon. "He said he works most nights and he was just heading out, so I arranged for us to meet for a late lunch tomorrow."

I still couldn't believe it. "He agreed to that?"

"Yes, and Jacob's off so I'm going to ask him to come with us."

I followed Ellen while she wobbled and then dropped to crawl around the kitchen table. "This might be weird," I said. "Jesse is Ellen's uncle, you know."

"I know," Diana replied thoughtfully, "and I'm pretty sure that's why he agreed to meet us."

I bent forward, scooped Ellen into my arms and gave her a raspberry on the belly. She shrieked with laughter.

"But where will this go?" I asked. "I hope we're not making a mistake. I feel like it's a risk because, like you said, we don't know anything about him."

"No," Diana replied, "but something tells me this is the right thing to do. I don't know why, but I had a gut feeling when I heard his voice. Otherwise I wouldn't have suggested we meet."

Ellen squirmed in my arms so I set her back down on the floor.

"And you've learned never to ignore a gut feeling," I mentioned. "So let's cross our fingers that this doesn't backfire. It would really suck if he turned out to be an axe murderer."

Chapter Thirty-two

"He's not going to show," I said to Diana as I checked my watch for the tenth time.

Diana and Jacob each checked their phones. "He's only five minutes late," Jacob said, "and traffic's always slow when it rains."

The three of us were seated around a square table in Imagination—a downtown restaurant known for its creative main-course salads. I'd chosen to leave Ellen at home with a sitter because I didn't feel comfortable introducing her to Rick's estranged brother when we knew so little about him.

The waitress came by and refilled our water glasses. I checked my watch again. "It's ten after three," I said. "He's not going to show."

Just then the door opened and a man walked in. He paused to wipe a hand over his hair and whisk the rain drops away, then glanced around the restaurant, which was mostly empty except for the three of us and one other couple.

The hostess greeted him, then picked up a menu and escorted him to our table.

"It's him," I quietly said.

Jacob stood and turned when Jesse arrived.

"Am I in the right place?" Jesse asked.

"Yes." Jacob held out his hand to shake Jesse's. "This is Diana Moore and Nadia Carmichael. I'm Jacob Peterson."

Jesse looked to be about my age. He was slim with medium-brown hair, blue eyes, and a goatee at his chin.

When he finished shaking our hands, he removed his rain jacket and draped it on the back of his chair. Then he looked down at Nadia and me as he sat down. "You're twins," he said with some surprise.

"Yes," Diana replied. "Identical, though we weren't raised together. We didn't even know about each other until two years ago."

"No kidding." The corner of Jesse's mouth curled up in a smile. "How did that happen?"

"It's a long story," Diana said, "but here's the condensed version. We were separated at birth and put up for adoption. Then by some miracle we ended up in the same city, working only a few blocks away from each other."

"Wow," he said, "that does sound like a miracle."

There was an awkward silence while Jesse glanced back and forth between the two of us. "So which one of you is—"

"The mother of Rick's baby?" I finished for him. Raising my hand, I said, "That would be me."

Our eyes met and held for the first time and he regarded me with curiosity, as if there were a hundred questions he wanted to ask. "So you're Nadia…."

I nodded, and felt a little flustered.

"I'm sorry," he said, "my head is spinning right now. This is strange."

"My head is spinning too," I replied. "It's been a weird couple of days."

I was referring not only to the news of Rick's custody suit, but also to the letter I'd received from my donor's family. But Jesse didn't know anything about my heart transplant and I wanted to keep it that way for now. There were other, more important things to discuss.

"You didn't bring your daughter with you?" he asked.

Diana leaned forward. "No, we wanted to meet you first."

He turned to her. "I see. To make sure I pass the litmus test?"

She shrugged. "Well…I'm sure you can understand…"

"Of course," he replied. "You don't know anything about me. I don't know anything about you, and this is all a bit strange."

There was a sudden tension in the air.

"Yes, it is," I replied. "And I'm sorry we caught you off guard. It must have been a surprise to hear from Diana, and I'm sure you're not exactly comfortable with the idea of talking to us, because Rick is your brother and you don't even know us. But I love my daughter, Mr. Fraser, and I need to do everything I can to—"

He held up a hand to stop me from completing the sentence. "First of all," he said, "call me Jesse. And second, let's not waste each other's time here. You don't want to lose custody of your daughter, and I get that. So what is it, exactly, that you need from me? Because whatever it is, I'll give it to you." He picked up his water glass and reclined in his chair. "Just tell me what happened between you and my brother. And what's he asking for?"

Chapter Thirty-three

I nearly sprayed my water out on the table because I didn't expect it to be this easy. His reply absolutely thrilled me. Diana's reaction wasn't quite the same, however. She frowned and sat forward.

"How long has it been since you've spoken to your family, Jesse?"

Great. Let's cross examine the witness. He might be hostile.

"About a decade," he replied.

She paused. "Can you tell us why you lost touch?"

He gazed at her for a moment. "Are you Nadia's lawyer as well as her sister?"

"Today I am," she replied. "But when this goes to court she'll be represented by a colleague of mine because there's a slight conflict of interest here."

Slight?

"How so?" he asked.

I kicked Diana under the table, because I didn't want to air our dirty laundry this early in the game. Jesse had just agreed to help us. I didn't want him to change his mind. But Diana ignored me.

"I'm the reason Nadia got involved with Rick in the first place," she explained. "He and I were seeing each other in LA when I found out Nadia was my twin. Then after I met Nadia,

Rick and I broke up. I moved back here to the east coast, and he and Nadia started seeing each other."

That was tactful, but she left out all the juicy bits.

For a long moment Jesse said nothing, then he turned his eyes to meet mine and spoke with understanding. "My brother's a real charmer, isn't he?"

I had the distinct impression Jesse knew—or at least suspected—that the situation had been far more complicated than Diana let on. What he didn't know was that all hell had broken loose when Rick kissed me in a hotel elevator while he and Diana were still a couple. When the elevator doors opened, there stood my sister in the lobby, staring at us with a look of shock and horror I will never forget.

The whole situation had been sordid and ugly, and to this day I am still surprised she was able to forgive me.

"He's only charming at first," I said to Jesse, to make it clear I had come to my senses. Eventually.

The waitress arrived to take our orders and when she left, another awkward silence ensued.

Jacob reached for Diana's hand. "What do you do, Jesse?" he politely asked. "Diana mentioned you work nights."

"I'm a helicopter pilot," he replied.

My eyebrows lifted. "That sounds exciting."

"Sometimes it is," he said. Then he smiled at me. "But sometimes it's not."

Jacob and Diana laughed and nodded. "I think it's safe to say that about any profession."

"And what do you do, Nadia?" Jesse asked me.

My stomach turned over because I had never done much of anything in my life—until I gave birth to Ellen and survived a heart transplant.

"I'm not working right now," I explained. "I had some health problems recently, and then of course Ellen came along. I'm just happy to be a stay-at-home mom at the moment."

I avoided mentioning the cause of my health problems because part of me was worried that if Jesse knew the risk factors I dealt with every day, he might change his mind about helping me keep full custody of Ellen.

"And what do you do?" Jesse asked Jacob.

"I'm a cardiac surgeon at Boston Mass," Jacob replied.

"I can't imagine *that* ever gets boring."

"It keeps me on my toes most days," Jacob said pleasantly.

One thing about Jacob—he was always very humble. He wasn't one of those arrogant doctors who walked around beating their chest.

"So I guess that's enough chit chat," Jesse said. Then he turned to Diana. "You asked why I hadn't spoken to my family in ten years, Ms. Moore, and I'm happy to tell you. I just don't know if it'll be of any help because it was such a long time ago."

Diana sat forward. "We'll appreciate any information you can give us."

Chapter Thirty-four

Jesse told us about a girl he had once loved—her name was Angela—and how Rick had stolen her away and gotten her pregnant. Rick then threatened to leave her if she didn't agree to an abortion, so she performed one on herself and bled to death in his bathroom. Jesse was the one who found her.

The waitress brought our meals just as he finished describing the events, but none of us could eat. We all sat in silence.

"I'm sorry that happened," I softly said.

Then I thought about how Rick had withdrawn from me so completely when I told him I was pregnant, and how he'd accused me of trying to trap him. How he pressured me to take the money and go away.

Now I saw how irresponsible he had been. In so many ways... on so many levels. Yet he made the women feel at fault, as if what happened had not involved him at all.

At least he never asked me to have an abortion. Now I knew why.

Jesse picked up his fork and we all began to eat, but the mood was somber.

"Did your parents know what happened?" Diana asked.

Jesse nodded. "I told them everything when I flew home, but they'd already talked to Rick and heard his side of the story. They implied it was my fault she did what she did—that if I had stayed out of it she would've gone to the hospital like she and Rick had decided and she'd be alive today."

I was horrified to hear that his parents would suggest such a thing. "You can't blame yourself," I said.

His eyes lifted and met mine. "I try not to." He ate slowly. "My parents swept everything under the carpet. They didn't attend Angela's funeral and they defended Rick to other people. They basically threw me under the bus, and that's why I haven't spoken to them or my brother in ten years."

Diana and I exchanged glances.

"Rick never mentioned any of that to us," I said. "But he was pretty up front about not wanting to get married or have kids."

"Not at first," Diana reminded me. "He always said everything I wanted to hear. He presented himself as perfect husband material and I honestly thought we'd end up together."

Jesse seemed to be listening, but he offered no response.

"I tried calling him after I received the lawyer's letter," Diana said, "but his phone was disconnected. We're wondering if he might be involved with someone new and maybe that's why he wants Ellen."

I moved my salad around on my plate. "Maybe he finally met the *right* woman who would be a perfect mother and he's a changed man."

Diana gave me a look. "There's no point speculating. I'll be talking to his lawyer soon enough."

Jesse reached for his water. "I'm sorry I can't be of more help, but I really have no idea what's going on in Rick's life these days. You probably know more than I do."

"Probably," I replied, "but what we do know seems consistent with the brother you just described, so it doesn't sound like he's changed much."

Jacob's cell phone rang. He reached into his pocket to check the call display. "Sorry," he said, "but I have to take this." He stood up and left the table to answer it. A few minutes later he returned. "That was the hospital and I have to go. Do you need a ride back to work?" he asked Diana.

"I have my umbrella," she said. "I can walk."

"You're sure?"

"Yes, you go ahead."

He gave her a kiss on the cheek, shook Jesse's hand and said, "It was nice meeting you." Then he hurried out the door into the driving wind and rain.

"Do you work nearby?" Jesse asked Diana. "Because I can give you a lift."

"I wouldn't want to trouble you," she said.

"It's no trouble." Then he turned to me. "Where are you headed, Nadia?"

I wiped my lips with the linen napkin. "I have to get home to Ellen. We live in Beacon Hill."

It didn't occur to me until after I spoke the words that Diana had arranged for us to meet Jesse downtown for a reason, and I had just upset that turnip cart by revealing where we lived.

"I'd be happy to give you a ride too," he said, "if you need one."

I met Diana's gaze and she shrugged, as if she was no longer concerned that he might be an axe murderer.

"That would be nice," I said. "Thank you." Then Diana asked the waitress to bring the check.

After we dropped Diana off at her office, Jesse headed toward Beacon Hill and I found myself rambling on and on, confessing all my doubts and concerns about the situation with Rick.

"It's tough because he's Ellen's father, and ethically and legally I don't have the right to keep him from seeing her. It's not like he has a criminal record or anything and he certainly wasn't abusive toward me or Diana. He just didn't want the responsibility of a family. He didn't want to marry me and I can't blame him for that. I'm no picnic. Not that I'm chopped liver or anything, but you know, sometimes it just doesn't work out. It happens all the time and who am I to tell Ellen that she can't know her father? If I tried to keep her from seeing him, I'm sure when she got older she'd resent me, and I don't want that either. So maybe I'm just going to have to accept that I'm not her only parent, and Rick has rights too."

Jesse glanced at me. "Sounds like you already have this figured out."

I shook my head. "Oh no. Not by a long shot. He lives on the other side of the country, so how is that going to work? He wants full custody. It feels like a war with all sorts of little battles to fight in different places, and I really don't feel up to that right now. It's been a rough year."

I gazed out the rain-soaked window and listened to the sound of the tires swishing through puddles on the streets.

"How so?" Jesse asked.

I don't know why I suddenly felt a need to clam up when I'd been blathering on for the past five minutes, but something kept me from telling him about my surgery. Maybe I'd simply shared enough for one day.

I turned my gaze to meet his and he stared at me for a few seconds.

"Never mind," he said. "It's none of my business."

Was I that easy to read?

I shrugged, as if to make light of it. "It's no big deal. I just never expected to be a single mother. It wasn't exactly what I planned, you know?"

He nodded.

"So what about you?" I asked, needing to change the subject. "Do you have kids?"

"No." He grinned at me. "But not for lack of trying."

Baffled and somewhat amused by his response, I laughed. "I'm not sure how to take that."

He flicked the blinker and turned left at an intersection with a flashing green light. "Me neither. I guess I've had a rough year, too."

Suddenly, my interest in Jesse Fraser quadrupled. As I watched his profile in the hazy gray light, I noted that he looked nothing like Rick, who was ridiculously charming and classically handsome with his striking dark features.

Jesse didn't possess the same whack-you-over-the-head charisma. He had a quieter personality and far less striking coloring and facial features. It was almost difficult to believe they were brothers.

He turned to glance at me and began to explain the rough year he'd had. "I was with a woman for five years and I proposed more than once, but she was never sure. We finally agreed to pack it in and move on." He paused. "Well, *she* agreed to move on. If it had been up to me, we'd be married right now with a kid on the way."

The wipers snapped vigorously back and forth across the windshield. "I'm sorry to hear that," I said. "Sometimes, love sucks."

"Tell me about it."

He turned onto my street and I pointed. "Keep going a little further. Just a bit more. I live right there. The one with the flowers in the window boxes. They're getting a good soaking today."

Jesse pulled over and I reached for my purse on the floor. "This was really nice of you," I said. "Not just the ride home, but for meeting us today."

"I don't know how helpful I was," he said. "Everything I know about Rick is old news, over a decade old. And people change."

I locked eyes with him. "Do you really believe that?"

"Of course."

"Then why haven't you spoken to him? Or to your parents?"

He inclined his head. "Good point, Nadia. And why haven't they spoken to *me*?"

I smiled. "We could go back and forth with this all day."

"But we won't," he replied with a grin, "because you have a baby to get home to."

I smiled. "Yes." I opened the door to step out, but halted when my foot landed on the wet curb. I pulled my leg back in and quickly shut the door.

"She's your niece, you know."

"I know that," he replied. "That's why I agreed to meet you today."

I paused. "Did you think I was going to bring her?"

He tapped his thumbs on the steering wheel. "I didn't know."

Maybe it was foolish of me—which was nothing new because I had made more than a few stupid decisions in my life—but I reached out and touched Jesse's arm. "Would you like to meet her now?"

His eyes clouded over with intensity, then he shut off the car engine and unbuckled his seatbelt. "Yeah, I would."

Chapter Thirty-five

Ellen was a child who thrived on routine, so it came as no surprise to me that she was asleep in her crib when we walked through the door.

I paid the sitter, thanked her, and said good-bye at the door, then I took Jesse's coat and hung it on the hall tree.

"She probably won't wake up for another hour," I said, "so can I offer you a cup of coffee? Or you could come upstairs with me now while I check on her."

"Really? If you don't mind…?"

"Not at all. She's so cute when she's sleeping but we'll have to be quiet. We'll tiptoe."

Was I mad, inviting a perfect stranger into my bedroom when there was no one else in the house? Probably. But for some reason I couldn't yet explain, I trusted this man.

I led the way and he followed me up the creaky stairs. "We share a room," I told him when we reached the top. "This is actually Diana's house but she lets me stay here. I don't know what I'd do without her."

When we reached my room, I was relieved to see that I had made my bed that morning and there were no clothes or toys flung about.

Together we approached the crib and looked in on Ellen who was sprawled on her back in her light pink pajamas. She looked so adorable I wanted to scoop her up in my arms and slobber all over her.

I gripped the top of the crib rail. "There she is. I love to watch her sleep."

He stared at her for a moment. "She's beautiful."

We didn't stay too long before we quietly tiptoed back downstairs.

"I can still make some coffee," I said when we reached the bottom, "if you want to stay until she wakes up."

"I'd love a coffee if it's not too much trouble," he replied.

"Not at all."

He followed me into the kitchen and I withdrew the grounds from the cupboard, then scooped them into the top of the coffee maker.

"I suppose someone who does shiftwork must drink a lot of coffee," I said.

"I don't mind working nights," he replied, "if I can stick to that schedule for a while. Your body gets used to it. It's when they move you around from days to nights...That's when it's rough."

I filled the coffee maker with water and pushed the start button. Then I pulled two mugs from the shelf. "Cream or sugar?"

"Just milk," he replied.

I retrieved the milk from the fridge and set everything on the table, then leaned against the counter to wait while the coffee brewed.

Jesse sat down and picked up the saltshaker that was in the shape of a bird house. He examined it briefly, then set it down and said, "I really can't understand how my brother—how *any* man—wouldn't want to know his own child. Your sister said he gave you money to stay away? He asked you never to contact him again?"

"Money and a car," I explained. "Which is why I was surprised to get his petition this week."

Jesse shook his head. "He and I were always very different. He would flit from one girl to another and I don't think he ever had his heart broken. Not while I knew him. Meanwhile, I always had a hard time letting go. I never wanted to lose anyone."

The coffee pot gurgled noisily and then grew quiet. I poured two cups and carried them to the table.

"It makes you wonder about nature versus nurture," I said. "You and Rick share the same genes, were raised in the same house by the same parents, yet your personalities and how you interact with people turned out to be very different. Diana and I were born as twins, reared apart, and our lives had very little in common when we met, yet deep down, I think we're alike. I guess at the end of the day every person is unique, and how they respond to their environment can vary."

Jesse poured some milk into his coffee. "I've often thought about that too. But all the pondering in the world can't help me understand how Rick could send you away like he did, or how he could have treated Angela the way he did all those years ago—and then not even go to her funeral." He shook his head. "I thought I was over it, but seeing your daughter just now...*His* daughter..." Jesse slowly sipped his coffee.

"I know," I said. "There's a resemblance there."

"The dark hair," he said.

I poured milk into my own cup. "Not to complicate matters, but here's my next question: Can a leopard change its spots? Because suddenly Rick wants to be involved and I don't feel the least bit equipped to fight him."

Jesse's eyes lifted. "Why not? Your sister's a lawyer."

"Yes, but I mean...emotionally. Ethically."

He leaned back in his chair to wait for me to elaborate.

"Remember when Diana mentioned that we were separated at birth?" He nodded and I continued. "Well I was born with a heart defect that couldn't be repaired right away, so I wasn't adopted until I was four years old. Unfortunately that situation wasn't ideal either and my father left us a few years later. I never saw him again. My adoptive mother died of lung cancer when I was nineteen and I never knew a single blood relative of my own until Diana contacted me. Now I have a child of my own and I don't want her to ever be without a family. I don't want her to be abandoned like I was. Rick is her natural father. Isn't blood thicker than water? I don't want to deny her that. Or deny *him* for that matter. Shouldn't I give him a chance?"

Jesse stared at me with concern. "Are you still in love with him?"

"No!" I blurted out. "Good Lord. It's not that."

"Are you sure?"

"Of course I'm sure."

He sipped his coffee again and watched me over the rim of the cup.

"I'm thinking of Ellen's future," I explained. "I want her to have lots of family, not just me, because all I had was my mom, and when she died I was left alone. At least until Diana showed up." I paused. "Do you understand?"

"I do," he quietly replied.

The lights on the baby monitor flickered and I heard Ellen begin to chatter.

"She's awake." I set down my coffee mug. "Wait here. I'll go get her and bring her down."

Chapter Thirty-six

"You invited him in?" Diana asked when she arrived home from work that evening. I was in the kitchen, feeding Ellen in her high chair. "Are you sure that was wise?"

"Why wouldn't it be?" I asked. "Didn't you think he was okay at lunch? Because I really liked him. I had a good feeling about him and remember what you said about never ignoring a gut feeling." I handed Ellen her spoon, hoping she'd eat some mashed potatoes but she patted them down with her hands.

Diana stood over us. "How did it go, then?" she asked. "Did he stay long?"

"About an hour," I replied. "Ellen was sleeping when we arrived so I made coffee. When she woke up I introduced them and we played with her in the living room until he had to go to work. We listened to some music and Jesse played elevator with her."

"What's *elevator*?" Diana asked.

"It was so cute," I explained. "He lifted her up, high over his head, gently set her down, then lifted her up again. And get this, she told him her blue blanket had a name. She calls it Ouwix."

"*Ouwix*!" Ellen said, raising her arms over her head.

"That's your blanket, isn't it!" I excitedly replied.

She laughed and nodded.

Diana smiled and sat down. "That is definitely cute. Here, let me finish with her."

I handed Diana the spoon and stood to go load the dishes into the dishwasher.

"He's certainly different from Rick," Diana said.

"Yeah. He's much more down to earth. Do you know he works for an air ambulance company? He flies rescue helicopters. Remember that kid that fell through the ice with his dog last winter? We saw it on the news and it went viral on YouTube? That was Jesse flying the bird that lowered the basket and pulled both of them out."

"Really? Wow, he didn't tell us that." Diana paused. "But just remember we still don't know that much about him and you have to be really careful right now. Your evaluation is coming up. It's important that you make the right impression."

"You mean it's important that I don't have a revolving door with a string of new men coming in and out of Ellen's life."

She glanced up at me. "Not that I think you would do that, but yes, that's what I mean. Appearances are everything."

"So I'm not allowed to have a boyfriend?"

She handed the spoon to Ellen again, and this time Ellen hung onto it and stirred her potatoes and meat. Diana turned in the chair to face me. "Is that where you see this going? You only met Jesse today."

Hearing the concern in her tone I plugged the sink, ran the water and squeezed the plastic dish detergent bottle. "Is this going to become one of your judgmental moments where you lecture me about not being an idiot?"

"No," she defensively replied. "I just want to know what to expect after today."

"You don't need to expect anything."

For the first time since I moved to Boston I wished I had my own place because suddenly I felt like a teenager who had to follow house rules. But I was in no position to complain. I was a single mother. I had no job, no money and I'd have no help with childcare if Diana wasn't a part of my life. I reminded myself how much she had done for me. I might not even be alive without her.

"He came in for coffee," I said. "That's all. And he was curious about Ellen because she's his niece. Wouldn't you be curious in his shoes?"

"I suppose." She turned around to help Ellen finish her supper while I dipped the plastic cups and bowls into the bubbly hot water to wash them.

Though I was grateful to Diana for everything she did for me, I was still annoyed with her for not trusting me to behave responsibly. At the same time, I found myself smiling as I remembered how Jesse had played hide-and-seek with Ellen that afternoon, and how she had laughed until she rolled over on the floor, kicking her legs.

Later Diana went over to Jacob's house and I was left home alone.

After I put Ellen to bed, I made some organic popcorn on the stove and stayed up late reading a romance novel.

When Ellen woke me the following morning, I was surprised to discover a text that had come in at 3:00 a.m. It was from Jesse, and just like that romance novel, it caused my new heart to flutter like crazy.

Chapter Thirty-seven

Are you free today? I'd like to talk to you about something.

I rolled over onto my back in bed and texted a reply: Yes, I'm free. What time and where?

I waited a few seconds to see if he would text back right away and he did: You're up early. Just heading to bed. 2:00?

Sure. Can Ellen join us? I usually take her for a walk in the afternoon.

He texted back a few seconds later: Yes to Ellen joining us. I'll come to your place at 2:00.

See you then! I replied.

Feeling exhilarated, I set my phone down and got out of bed to fetch Ellen who was standing up in her crib, waiting for me to lift her out.

"Good morning, sunshine!" I said. "Weatherman says it's going to be a beautiful day."

I lowered the crib rail. She grabbed hold of her blanket and dragged it with her as I lifted her into my arms.

For some reason, I chose not to tell Diana about my meeting with Jesse that afternoon. I wanted to find out what he wanted to talk about first.

He knocked on my door at 2:00 on the nose and I invited him in to wait while I put sunscreen on and buckled Ellen into her stroller. He helped me lift her down the steps to the street.

"How was work last night?" I asked as I handed Ellen a sippy cup full of diluted apple juice before adjusting the brim of her sunhat.

"Uneventful," he replied. "I spent most of the night in the hangar dealing with the engineers. There was a problem with a gearbox."

"What's a gearbox?" I asked, gripping the stroller handle and pushing off.

"A very important piece of machinery," he explained as he fell into step beside me. "It sends power from the engine to the rotors."

"The rotors are the blades that keep you in the air?"

"That's right."

"Ah," I said. "That does sound important." We chatted more about his work, reached the end of the street and headed toward the Public Garden.

"You said, in your text, that you wanted to talk to me about something?" I casually asked him.

"Yeah," he replied, "though it's nothing specific. It's just... After meeting you and Ellen yesterday, I can't stop thinking about your custody case. I'm surprised Rick is doing this. It brought back some memories."

"Your girlfriend?" I gently said.

He nodded and gestured with his hands. "I want to *help* you. You said you couldn't get hold of Rick. What if I called my parents to try and find out where he is? I don't even know if they're aware of what's happening. Or maybe they put him up to this for all I know."

I gazed up at Jesse with bewilderment. "You said you hadn't spoken to your parents in ten years. Why would you want to do that for me? You hardly know me."

Jesse slipped his hands into the pockets of his jeans and slid me a glance. "You seem like a nice enough person and I saw how you were with your daughter yesterday. You're a good mom and I can't stomach the idea of my brother taking Ellen away from you."

As I pushed Ellen's stroller along the brick sidewalk, I remembered Diana's advice to me about the dangers of inviting men into my life when the courts were judging my fitness as a single parent. Yet nothing could stop the thrilling spark of excitement that flared inside me when Jesse said those kind words.

He squinted up at the sky. "I've seen Rick do too many things without a single thought for how others might feel. He was like that when we were young, especially with girls. I don't know how he lived with himself."

Diana was right about something else—Jesse was nothing like Rick. He was a kinder, gentler soul. I had known few men like him in my life.

Though I'd only met Jesse the previous day, I could easily see myself falling head over heels in love with him—which was a dangerous thing because I needed to stay focused on Ellen and the custody suit.

We entered the Public Garden at the corner of Beacon and Charles Streets and walked leisurely down the wide path toward the lagoon. As we entered the shade beneath a large silver maple, I gazed up at the leaves, listened to the sound of Ellen's squeaky stroller wheels and breathed in the fresh scent of the late summer air.

It was moments like these when I became almost overcome by the rapture of simply being alive. I thanked God for the miracle of modern medicine and the generosity of my organ donor.

I wanted to share my joy with Jesse, but something held me back. Maybe it was the fact that I sensed a brewing attraction between us. Was I worried it might change how he felt about me if he knew there was a long disfiguring scar between my breasts?

Really...what man would knowingly become involved with a woman who was constantly at risk for infections and had to take medications for the rest of her life to prevent her body from rejecting her own heart?

It was because of the scar that I didn't wear low cut tank tops, even in this scorching summer heat. I preferred to keep it hidden from view.

We reached a giant weeping willow and I heard the calming sound of the ducks quacking on the water.

"Have you ever taken Ellen for a ride on one of the Swan Boats?" Jesse asked.

I smiled up at him. "Not yet, but it's been on my To Do list since the start of the summer."

"We should go," he suggested. "We'll pretend to be tourists."

"All right," I replied with a laugh, knowing better than anyone that life was precious and opportunities like this shouldn't be squandered.

Together, we headed over to the boat dock to buy our tickets.

It was a fifteen-minute ride around the Lagoon with a college-aged captain who sat in the swan seat at the rear of the boat and peddled us around. We passed slowly under the bridge, past weeping willows with branches dipping into the water. Ellen loved seeing the real swans that peddled faster than we did and overtook us around the bend.

When we returned to the dock and stepped off the boat, I laughed with Jesse that it was the best two dollars and seventy-five cents I'd ever spent. He made sure to remind me with a playful nudge that he had been the one to pay for the tickets.

Soon we were strolling along the wide path again. Jesse wanted to know more about how Diana and I found each other in Los Angeles two years ago.

"It must have been strange to meet your identical twin for the first time," he said.

I told him everything—how she'd contacted me in a letter and how we exchanged emails back and forth, then finally met in a nearby restaurant.

"I used to have a recurring dream," he told me, "that I was running beside myself around a race track. Kind of like I was looking at my twin and cheering him on. I never knew what it meant. I still don't."

"I have a recurring dream too," I said. "I dream that I'm flying, usually at night."

"Really? I think that's a pretty common dream for people." He pulled out his phone. "Let's Google it and see what it means."

He typed in the question as we walked, then cupped a hand over the screen to shade it from the sunlight.

"Here we go," he said. "This is from Dream Moods dot com. It says 'If you are flying with ease and are enjoying the scene and landscape below, then it suggests that you are on top of a situation. You have risen above something. It may also mean that you have gained a new and different perspective on things. Flying dreams and the ability to control your flight is representative of your own personal sense of power.'" He lowered his phone and looked at me. "Do you fly with ease?"

I thought about it. "Yeah, I do. I'm not scared or afraid of heights and I always feel pretty good when I wake up, as if I had a good time exploring new places."

He nodded. "Well, it's very clear to me that you have risen above something and I admire you for it."

I inclined my head at him. "What's that?" I asked.

Had he caught a glimpse of my scar somehow? Did he know the truth? Maybe at lunch, I'd leaned the wrong way and my blouse had fallen open slightly.

Then he smiled. "You kicked my good-for-nothing brother to the curb."

There was no mistaking the flirtatious glimmer of amusement in his eye and I felt a rush of excitement. "You're right. That has *got* to be my great accomplishment," I said with a laugh. "Now I understand!"

We continued walking and as I pondered the true meaning of my dreams, I realized they hadn't begun until about six or eight months after my transplant surgery—when I was finally on the road to a clean bill of health. It made perfect sense that I would feel victorious while I slept.

Suddenly I felt foolish for imagining it had anything to do with my donor. Had I truly contemplated contacting his family to suggest that the spirit of their lost loved one was inhabiting me, flying me over the hospital where he died? They surely would have thought I was a basket case.

Jesse helped me push the stroller onto a grassy knoll and I unbuckled Ellen so she could toddle around. She laughed as Jesse chased her. He caught her, lifted her up onto his shoulders and carried her to the edge of the Lagoon where they watched the ducks and Swan Boats. Then they played elevator again.

I stayed behind with the empty stroller and wondered what the future held for Ellen and me. Here we were, spending the afternoon with a man who was her uncle by blood—a man I found immensely attractive. A man I already trusted in a way that surprised me.

Meanwhile his brother, who had caused Diana and me great pain and heartache in the past, was suing for custody.

Our broken hearts were insignificant, of course, compared to the thought of losing my daughter who I loved with all my heart. Ellen was the whole world to me, the sole purpose for my existence. She was my reason for living, for surviving. I couldn't lose her. I simply couldn't.

Though Rick had been the one to give her to me, I hated him in that moment. Did he know the level of pain he would inflict if he took her away?

Did he care? Was he even capable of caring?

According to Jesse, probably not.

Perhaps that was how I would prove I was the better parent.

Revisiting the Past

Chapter Thirty-eight

Jesse Fraser

I began this story with a query about coincidences, but I'm not entirely certain that what happened to me could be called such a thing. Everything seemed so orchestrated, as if a puppet master stood over us plotting our movements, moving us here and there, back and forth across a stage. It all came together so tidily in the end that it seemed predestined, as if someone had programed our lives to intersect at a certain moment in time, so a deeper, more profound knowledge would come to all of us.

But I'm not sure you'll believe in that sort of thing.

When I first met Nadia Carmichael, I was the most unromantic skeptic who ever lived. I was jaded and guarded when it came to women, yet my heart nearly exploded out of my chest when she looked up at me for the first time in the restaurant… with her big, expressive eyes.

I don't know why I reacted that way to her when I was meeting her identical twin at the same moment. Why was I so powerfully drawn to Nadia and not Diana?

I suppose I'll never know unless I admit to believing in love at first sight, or soul mates, or recognizing people you know from some other lifetime or dimension. Or maybe it was just chemistry. Hormones and pheromones.

Whatever the case, when I sat down at that table for lunch with Nadia, Diana and Dr. Jacob Peterson, my fate was sealed. There was no getting out of it. I simply had to help this woman keep her child.

I just wasn't sure *why* I needed to help her. Or what my true motivation was.

Even when I sent the text to Nadia in the middle of the night—twelve hours after we first met—I was still unsure of my purpose. I had grappled with the decision to see her again and had told myself it was a bad idea.

Don't text her. Stay out of it.

Hadn't she made her bed when she made the mistake of falling for my brother's charms? This wasn't my problem. Was I to spend my entire life cleaning up the emotional wreckage in every woman my brother left behind? Was that even possible? I certainly hadn't been able to save Angela.

But was *that* what I was trying to do? *Save* Nadia? Did I even have the power to do that? What if I somehow made things worse?

Nevertheless, despite all my angst, self-doubt and clumsy decision-making, I sent the text and arranged to meet her.

Then, true to form, I became even more infatuated. So infatuated in fact, that in the first five minutes during our walk to the Garden, I promised I would call my parents and track down my brother. I would find out what I could to help her case.

Was I mad? Yes.

Did I regret it? Definitely not.

Here's what I learned…

"Dr. Fraser speaking."

The sound of my father's quiet baritone voice on the phone was like a slingshot that sent me straight back to my childhood, to the memory of how he could walk into a room and intimidate me with just one look.

You'll never be quite as good as your brother.

That was the look. I could see it on his face now.

"Dad," I said as I settled into a chair, "it's Jesse."

My greeting was met with silence.

"Are you there?" I asked.

My father cleared his throat. "Yes, I'm here. Well. This is a surprise."

I'd never heard my father sound flustered before, but there was always a first time for everything.

"How are you?" I asked. "How's Mom?"

"She's well," he replied. "And you?"

I almost wanted to laugh. I was his youngest son and he hadn't heard from me in a decade. To my knowledge he didn't even know if I was dead or alive unless he had somehow been keeping tabs on me. Yet he spoke as if I called to confirm an appointment for a dental cleaning. I kept waiting for him to suggest I call his receptionist back in the morning.

"I'm all right," I replied. "You're probably wondering why I'm calling."

"Yes. Should I get your mother on the phone?"

"That would be great," I said.

"Just a second. I'll get her." He must have set the phone down and walked away because I heard nothing for a moment or two. Then a click told me that someone else had joined the call.

"Jesse?" The sound of my mother's voice compared to my father's had quite the opposite effect on me. Joy poured through me and I wanted desperately to see her in person.

"Yes, Mom, it's me," I said. "It's good to hear your voice."

"It's good to hear yours, too," she replied. Her warmth and affection reached me through the phone line. I knew, without a doubt, that the emotion was genuine. "Where are you?" she asked. "Still working in Boston?"

So they *had* been keeping tabs on me.

"Yes," I replied. "I'm piloting for a private medevac company."

"Planes or helicopters?" she asked.

"Helicopters."

"I see." She paused. "You're always careful, I hope. I know how dangerous that job can be."

"I'm careful, Mom," I assured her.

"I'm glad to hear it. Are you seeing anyone? Do you have a girlfriend? You're not married yet, are you?"

"No," I replied with a smile and wondered why I had waited so long to call her. This wasn't what I had expected…until my father spoke up.

His voice was like a sledgehammer, demolishing our conversation, reminding me why I left. "Why are you calling us, Jesse? Why now?"

The message that he had not forgotten or forgiven any of the angry words I had spoken years ago was received loud and clear. My mother grew quiet.

"I'm calling about Rick," I said, point blank. "I'd like to get in touch with him but his number isn't listed."

"That's because he recently moved," my father explained.

"I figured as much," I replied. "Do you have his new number?"

Neither of them answered my question, which made me wonder what the big secret was. "Are you afraid I'll call him up, stir up the past and threaten his life or something?" I asked.

"Of course not," Mom said. "But can you tell us what you want to talk to him about before we put you in touch?"

"Why?" I asked. "Do you feel you need to protect him from me?"

It was a ridiculous suggestion because Rick, of all people, enjoyed fighting his own battles. Though he'd always had our parents' support, they never knew what was *really* going on. He was one person with them, and quite another with me.

"Why do you want to call him, Jesse?" I was surprised by her accusing tone and by the fact that it was coming from her and not Dad. "Have you heard something?"

My eyebrows pulled together with confusion. Obviously there was something going on—but was it the custody suit or another matter?

"I did hear something," I replied. "I heard he's suing a woman for custody of their child."

There was a pause. "That's right."

"So you know about it?" I asked.

"Of course we know," my father scoffed. "We're the ones who encouraged him to seek custody."

I shut my eyes and cupped my forehead in a hand. "Why doesn't that surprise me?"

"I don't know what you're implying," Dad said, "but I don't like your tone."

I opened my eyes and dropped my hand to the armrest. "I don't like yours either, Dad, so I guess we're even on that score."

"Jesse, please…" Mom whispered. "I don't want this to turn into another argument."

"Then maybe Dad should hang up and I should just talk to you."

"I'm not hanging up," he announced. "If you want to know what's going on with your brother, I'll tell you. Not that you deserve to know, but since you made the effort to call…"

I sat forward and rested my elbows on my knees. "Yes I did make the effort. So tell me," I said. "Please."

Chapter Thirty-nine

When my mother explained the situation, her words vibrated through me. It took a few seconds for my brain to catch up. "My God," I said. "When did this happen?"

"It began about a year ago," Mom said. "He started having symptoms so he went to see his doctor. Before we knew it, he was having surgery. Then came the chemotherapy. That's what caused the sterility."

I couldn't believe it. My picture-perfect brother had been diagnosed with testicular cancer and now he was sterile.

Which explained why he suddenly wanted Ellen.

Or perhaps why my parents wanted her.

"So he'll never be able to have children of his own?" I asked. Despite everything, my heart felt heavy.

"Not unless he adopts," my father answered, "which he and Christine may decide to do in the future."

I felt a jolt. "Who's Christine?"

"His fiancée," Mom said. "They're getting married next month. That's why his phone was disconnected. They moved in together and he left his job, left everything behind. He truly wanted a fresh start. They're not in LA anymore."

My head drew back in surprise. "Rick is getting *married*? And he left LA?"

"Yes, isn't it wonderful? The doctor says he's completely cured. He beat the cancer and met the most wonderful girl. She's a physicist."

"How did they meet?" I asked, still reeling with shock, because Rick didn't usually go for the brainy types unless they were also gorgeous. Maybe Christine was a model on the side.

"At the hospital," she explained. "Christine's mother was being treated at the clinic at the same time as Rick. I'm sorry to say she has breast cancer, but she's a fighter. Anyway, you know Rick. He can't resist any opportunity to flirt with a pretty girl."

I massaged my temples. "No, I guess not. But are you sure he's going to go through with the wedding? You know how he has a tendency to…" I stopped myself. I didn't want to rain on my mother's happy parade when she had obviously been through so much.

"Yes, we're sure," she insisted. "I know you might find this difficult to believe, Jesse, but he's changed. This cancer scare—and meeting Christine—have made him see life differently. He was always very ambitious, professionally, but now he wants to be the best man he can be, to never take anything for granted. He wants to enjoy the simpler things and we're so proud of him."

"You always were," I reminded her.

She let out a sigh of defeat, as if she was disappointed that I had failed to understand how marvelous Rick was with his new lease on life. "Yes," she said, "but we're even more proud of him now." She paused. "He's had time to think about what he's accomplished—and hasn't accomplished—and I won't lie. He has some regrets about certain things. Things that caused the rift between the two of you."

"You mean Angela," I said.

Another pause. "Yes. Rick agonized over that when he was having his treatments. That's when he told Christine about Ellen, and then she told us."

I wasn't about to say it out loud to my mother, but despite everything she'd just described, I still had a hard time believing that Rick truly regretted what happened to Angela or that he felt any genuine love for the infant daughter he'd never met. It wasn't that long ago that he cast Nadia out and paid her a generous sum of money to stay away and never ask him for anything more. To never force him to face up to his responsibilities, or to commit to one woman. To be a father.

Now that he had a clean bill of health, I wondered how long it would take for him to return to his old ways. Poor Christine would become dull and boring and he would suddenly wake up one morning and realize he wanted to live life to the fullest.

'So many women, so little time.' Wasn't that his favorite catch phrase in college?

What would happen to Ellen? What about Nadia?

I decided to probe a little further and ask my parents what they knew about Nadia. "Did Rick say much about his relationship with the mother?"

"Yes, he told us everything and we met her sister Diana when she was living with him. She seemed like a very nice woman at the time, but then Nadia came along—her identical twin—and..." Mom paused. "Oh, it's all very disturbing."

"How so?" I asked, growing more curious by the second.

"I'd rather not talk about it," Mom replied. "All I can say is that when Diana couldn't convince Rick to marry her—she was very pushy—the other one tried and she tricked him into getting her pregnant. She hoped to trap him. Obviously they were working together and were both after his money."

"What do you mean, *tricked*?" I asked. "Are you sure that's what happened?"

I still wasn't ready to believe whatever Rick said to our parents because I knew better than anyone how he could spin a tale to place himself in the most favorable light. He had a talent for shifting the blame.

"I'm quite sure," she replied. "He was very generous and gave her a financial settlement, and thank God the contract was iron clad. It prohibited her from asking for more and she signed it."

"But now Rick wants the baby," I said.

"Yes, and it makes perfect sense that he and Christine should be the ones to raise her. Everything has fallen into place so beautifully."

"Beautifully? Are you forgetting that the mother of that child doesn't want to lose her daughter?"

"I'm sure she doesn't," my father put in, "but any court with a sensible judge will rule for the benefit of the child—and Ellen would be far better off with Rick and Christine."

"How can you say that?" I asked. "You don't know Nadia at all. Is it because Rick has more money? Or is it because he's sterile now and suddenly he wants what he can't have? And whatever Rick wants, he should get?"

"No, Jesse," my father replied in a calm, patronizing tone. "It's because that woman is in very poor health and the child deserves to have a stable home with both a mother and a father."

"What are you talking about?" I asked. "What do you know about her?"

He was quiet for a moment. "We've looked into things and we know her life expectancy."

My gut began to churn. I frowned and sat forward. "I still don't understand."

"Nadia Carmichael had a heart transplant just after Ellen was born," my father explained, "so she'll always be at risk for infections. She'll be lucky to live fifteen years."

Unable to move, I stared at the wall, then I heard my mother saying, "*Jesse? Jesse, are you still there?*"

"Yes, I'm here." I slowly rose to my feet. "Thanks for telling me this. Can you give me Rick's number now? I'd like to call him."

"Of course," Mom said.

She read me his new number, and I wrote it down on a scrap of paper.

"I have to go," I said. "I'll call you again. I promise."

I hung up and strode to the kitchen to grab my keys.

Chapter Forty

"Jesse, this is a surprise." Diana stepped back and invited me inside. "Come on in."

"I should have called," I said as I entered her home. "I sent a text to Nadia but she didn't reply.

"She just got out of the shower," Diana said.

Just then, my phone vibrated. I pulled it out and checked the messages. "There's her reply," I mentioned.

Diana smiled. "I'll run up and tell her you're here." She started up the stairs. "Have a seat."

I moved into the living room where Ellen was bouncing in a colorful activity center.

"Hey there, what's up?" I knelt down in front of her. "This is quite the gizmo. They didn't make toys like this when I was your age." I couldn't help myself. I pushed each of the big, lighted buttons that played musical notes. Ellen giggled at me. Then I played around with the frog spinner. "What's this doohickey here?" I fiddled with the bead chaser next. "This is cool." I sat back on my heels. "It's kind of like your own little space ship."

"That's exactly what I thought when it was given to us." Nadia's voice startled me. I rose to my feet and turned around.

There she stood wearing a pair of denim shorts and a loose-fitting black T-shirt. Her long dark hair hung wet and wavy about her shoulders. She was drying the ends off with a towel. Her feet were bare.

Her beauty rendered me speechless and spellbound. At the same time, I was distracted by fact that she had recently undergone a heart transplant and survived it.

What else didn't I know about her?

I massaged the back of my neck with my hand.

"Sorry to barge in," I said, "but I didn't think it could wait."

Her eyebrows lifted. "Why? Did something happen?"

"Yeah. Do you have a minute?" I asked.

"Of course." She moved fully into the room and sat down on the sofa where she continued to squeeze the wet ends of her hair with the towel.

Nearby, Ellen bounced happily in her ExerSaucer.

"Maybe Diana should be here," I mentioned, "because this is about Rick."

"Oh." The color drained from Nadia's face. "Did you talk to your parents today?"

When I told her I had, Nadia called Diana into the room. Soon we were all seated around the coffee table. Nadia set the towel aside.

I wasted no time in explaining how Rick had been diagnosed with cancer a year ago and had surgery and chemotherapy.

Diana covered her mouth with a hand. "That's awful. I can't believe it. Is he okay?"

"He's fine now," I replied. "He made it through all the treatments and my parents say he's completely cured."

"What a relief." Diana was still in shock, while Nadia stared at Ellen with concern.

"I'm sorry to hear about it, too," she said. "What a year it's been…for all of us." She paused and met my gaze. "Is this why he wants to be a part of Ellen's life now? A brush with death can make you think about things."

Obviously she was speaking from experience. I looked down at my lap. "Yeah, but it's not just that. Unfortunately, the chemotherapy caused some trouble. He can't have children now."

Diana sat forward. "He's sterile?"

"Yes," I replied, "and he's engaged. Apparently he met someone when he was having his treatments—a woman whose mother was in for breast cancer treatments."

Nadia winced and covered her face with her hands. "Oh, God, I knew it. He has all his ducks in a row. What court is ever going to refuse him custody of his own child after all he's been through? And now he's going to be a perfect husband with a happy home and all the money in the universe."

"I wouldn't go that far," Diana said. "And it's not a lost cause yet. You're still Ellen's mother and you've been taking great care of her on your own. She's a happy, healthy little girl."

"Only because of *you*," I argued. "If not for you I'd be out on the street, or maybe even dead. I haven't been able to work for more than a year, and even if I could, how would I pay for childcare?"

Diana held up a hand. "That's not even an issue. You're my sister and this is your house, too. I've already named you as my sole beneficiary in my will, so all my assets go to you if I should die."

"But you support me completely, in every way," I said. "I'm not reliable on my own."

"Who *is*?" Diana argued. "Either way I'm here for you and I'm Ellen's guardian if anything should happen, so she's safe and she has everything she needs."

Nadia stood up and began to pace. I felt as if I was intruding on their conversation. I was a stranger in their home and they were discussing things I supposedly knew nothing about—although I did know something about it. I was going to have to say something soon.

Ellen began to cry, sensing the tension, no doubt. How could anyone miss it?

Nadia lifted Ellen out of the ExerSaucer. "There, there," she gently said. Holding her close in her arms, she stroked her baby's back and kissed her on the cheek. "Everything's going to be okay."

Diana pinched the bridge of her nose. I could see she was concerned about the case. She was a lawyer. She knew the facts and the odds. And she knew Rick.

Nadia looked down at me. "I'm sorry, Jesse. I'm sure you didn't expect the whole world to explode like this when you came here."

"Don't apologize," I said. "I get it."

Nadia paced around the room, whispering soothing words to Ellen. Quietly, she asked me, "Have you spoken to him at all?"

I shook my head. "Not yet, but I will if you want me to."

"What would you say?"

"I could try and talk some sense into him," I said. "I'll tell him how much you love Ellen and make him see that it would be wrong to take her away from you."

I didn't admit this to Nadia, but deep down I wasn't sure how much good it would do. Rick and I had never seen eye to eye on anything. He had never listened to me before, not when it came to the pain of others.

Diana looked up. "Jesse's right. We have to try and make Rick see that he's asking too much and it would be very cruel to Ellen." She took a moment to think about everything, then continued. "I'm sorry to say this, Nadia, but the truth is…after hearing this…there's very little chance we can prevent him from gaining custody, but it doesn't have to be *full* custody. If he, or his new fiancée, could only see you with Ellen, we might be able to convince them to consider a shared custody arrangement. Let's hope his fiancée is reasonable and that she has a kind heart."

Nadia scoffed. "What are the chances of that? I can just see her now. She wants a perfect life in a ritzy penthouse with a shiny black Jag. She can even have an instant baby without the problem of stretch marks. She'll crush me like a bug."

I turned in my chair. "According to my parents, she's a physicist and they said Rick left his job and moved out of LA. They bought a house in Sacramento."

Diana's eyes nearly popped out of her head. "Sacramento? Rick is living in Sacramento?"

I nodded and Nadia continued to pace. We were all quiet for a long moment.

"Maybe he really has changed," Diana suggested.

Nadia and I both looked at her like she'd grown a second head.

"Either way," she said, "we have to prepare ourselves. If he can suddenly present himself as the perfect father, we need to make sure you're the perfect mother."

Nadia sat down on the sofa and bounced Ellen on her knee. "I'm hardly that. You know I have a very big flaw."

She and Diana, identical twins on opposite ends of the sofa, shared an intimate look.

"Because you had a heart transplant?" I asked.

They each turned to me.

"You know about that?" Nadia asked.

I nodded. "My parents told me. And I'm pretty sure that's Rick's strongest argument against you."

"Of course it is." Diana seemed unsurprised.

Nadia stared at me with regret. "I'm sorry I didn't tell you about that."

"No worries," I replied. "You only just met me."

Diana stood and reached her arms out to Ellen. "Hey cutie pie, how about some supper?" She settled Ellen on her hip, then ventured toward the kitchen. "Why don't you two have a conversation about that? I'll feed Ellen and put her to bed."

With that, she left us alone.

We sat for a moment, staring at each other in silence. "Want to go for a drive?" I suggested.

"Sure," Nadia replied. "Just let me put on some shoes."

Chapter Forty-one

"I should have told you about the transplant," Nadia said as we pulled away from the curb, "but I didn't want you to feel sorry for me."

"*Sorry* for you?" I laughed at that. "Trust me, that's not what I'm feeling at all." I turned right at the corner and headed toward the Charles River Esplanade. "I'm amazed that you're alive, that you went through all of that and had Ellen, and now you're dealing with this custody case. What I really think is that you must be made of something incredibly...*durable*."

"Durable?" Nadia chuckled. "You see? This is exactly what I was trying to avoid, because no woman wants an attractive man to think of her as *durable*."

I kept my eyes on the road. "So you think I'm attractive..."

She laughed. "You're all right."

I smiled and pressed on the gas.

"So what happened?" I finally asked. "Can you tell me about it?"

She breathed deeply. "Are you sure you want to know?"

"I do."

We shared a look, then she rolled down the window. "I got sick when I was pregnant with Ellen. I was about five months along. It just seemed like a regular flu virus at first, nothing to be concerned about, but afterward, when I should have been getting better, I felt more and more tired. I was short of breath all the time. I thought maybe it was just the pregnancy because everyone told me it was normal to feel tired, but eventually I ended up in the hospital in heart failure."

"God…"

She nodded. "What I had is called myocarditis and it's not that uncommon. The virus attacks the heart muscle, so it had nothing to do with me eating fatty foods or not getting enough exercise. My heart was in perfect working order before that. It was just a run of bad luck, made worse by the fact that I was pregnant which took more of a toll on my body. But we were incredibly lucky, Ellen and I. I was able to hang on long enough for them to deliver her by C-section. Then I got lucky again with a donor heart that became available not long after. That was just under a year ago. Now I'm doing pretty well."

I glanced at Nadia in the passenger seat and though I didn't intend it, my gaze raked over the full length of her body. "You certainly *look* great."

Her expressive eyes shone in the pale light of the evening. "Shameless flatterer."

Something intense sparked between us, and nothing could have lessened my attraction to her—not a heart transplant, not the fact that we barely knew each other, and especially not my brother who still managed to maintain a cruel hold on her from miles away. If anything, that made me want to help her even more.

With that thought, I wondered—with more than a little unease—what was happening here, exactly?

There was no question that I had feelings for Nadia. How could I not? She was articulate, interesting and gorgeous. I could barely think straight when she was around and when she wasn't, all I wanted to do was find a way to be with her again.

But I also wanted to make sure Rick didn't destroy her like he destroyed Angela.

So was this about Rick, then? Would I still be here—would I be so drawn to this wounded woman—if it was some other man suing her for custody of their child? Or would I be running for the hills?

Dreams

Chapter Forty-two

Nadia

For me, the world came into focus on that hazy summer evening when Jesse took me driving and I told him about my heart transplant. That was the night I knew something extraordinary was truly happening between us and it wasn't just my imagination.

The whole interior of his car lit up with electricity every time we looked at each other. He asked intimate and caring questions and I quickly came to appreciate that he wasn't like other men who prefer to play it cool at first.

To the contrary, Jesse was an open book. He revealed his feelings to me in ways no other man ever had on a first or second date. I suspected he wouldn't be afraid to leap into a serious relationship right away. In fact, I believe, in those early days, that he desperately wanted it—that he felt he had loved and lost enough for one lifetime. I sensed that he craved permanence. When I was with him, I never felt I had to worry about coming on too strong, nor did I have to play games. He wanted to know everything about me that night. It continues to surprise me, as I look back on it.

Because for a man who wanted permanence and love to last a lifetime, I was, without a doubt, completely wrong for him.

"Would you have married Rick if he'd proposed?" Jesse asked after we parked the car and began to stroll along the bank of the Charles River. The sun was just setting and the sky glowed with a mixture of pinks and blues.

"You mean when I told him I was pregnant?" I gestured to a green painted bench where we sat down to watch the sailboats go by.

Jesse rested an arm along the back of the bench and waited for me to answer the question, but I really had to think about it. Not that I didn't already know the answer. I did, but I had to figure out how to articulate it.

Turning on the bench to face him, I was briefly distracted by the absorbing blue color of his eyes and the handsome contours of his face. The longer I knew him, the more attractive he became. I needed to keep my head, however, so I looked down at my hands in my lap.

"It's not easy to admit this," I replied, "but I think I might have said yes if he proposed. Not because I loved him or believed he would make a good husband or father. After what happened with Diana and me I didn't believe that at all, but I was alone and afraid and I wanted to take good care of my baby. Your brother had money, and that, on its own, might have been enough to sway me. It would have been a mistake, of course, and I'm sure I would have regretted it."

"Really?" he asked. "Would you regret it now if it meant you wouldn't be fighting a custody battle?"

"I would have had to fight one eventually," I told him. "It just would have been mixed in with a divorce."

He gazed out at the water and nodded. "How long were you together?"

"Not that long. Only a few months and I still blame myself for the fact that we ended up together at all. I'm not proud of it because he was with Diana before. I'm the reason they broke up."

"Is that true?"

"Yes, but you have to understand where I was coming from. I'd had a rough life until that point. I started out in foster homes, then I was adopted, but my dad wasn't a model parent. My mom died later, so when I met Rick I had no family, except for Diana, who I'd only just met. When he poured on the charm, I wasn't equipped to deal with it or turn him down. Like I said, I'm not proud of what happened and I thank God every day that Diana was able to forgive me."

We were quiet for a long moment while joggers ran by us and boats sailed slowly toward the mouth of the harbor.

"Have you ever thought about forgiving Rick for the things that happened between you?" I asked.

Jesse turned his body to face me again. "I'm surprised to hear that question from you of all people, because when it comes to Rick you have so much to lose."

"I do," I replied, "and I'm not suggesting that I intend to play nice and throw in the towel. But I also believe that people can change, especially when they face certain...*realities* in life."

"You mean death."

I nodded and lowered my gaze. "It opens your eyes."

He sat quietly, as if reliving different memories from his childhood.

"He and I were always so different," Jesse said. "I'm honestly not sure if his eyes can be opened. He's seen death before but it made no difference. It didn't soften him." He paused. "There's a lot of water under the bridge."

"Yes, but you were both young when those things happened. A person can learn a lot in ten years, especially when the death you're facing is your own. I'm sure you've changed, too."

"Not that much," Jesse said. "I was always too sensitive for my own good. But this isn't about me; it's about Rick and it wasn't that long ago that he sent you away. Was he by your side when you had your surgeries? I doubt it. Did he offer any support? Did he offer to take care of Ellen?"

"He's offering that now," I reminded him.

Jesse shook his head and I could see that he was nowhere near ready to forgive his brother. "*Offering* is a very polite word for it."

"Maybe you're right," I replied with a heavy sigh. "At the end of the day, I don't know what we're dealing with, but I don't want to burn any bridges either. If we're going to have to share custody of Ellen, I want to do that as peacefully as possible."

Jesse looked at me intently. "You *do* sound like you're giving up before you've even begun to fight."

"Maybe."

"Don't you believe it's possible that the judge might rule in your favor? That he could just award Rick visitation rights or something?"

I considered it. "I'm a single mother with serious health problems. So maybe *I'm* the selfish one, wanting to keep Ellen all to myself. Maybe she'd be better off with a mother and a father who will be around when she graduates from high school or when she walks down the aisle."

"You'll be around for those things," Jesse said, cupping my chin in his hand.

"How do you know?"

He stroked my cheek with his thumb and I wanted to melt into his arms.

"I guess I'm an optimist," he said with an encouraging smile. "Or maybe I should say I have a gut feeling."

I wet my lips. "Diana always tells me never to ignore a gut feeling. She also keeps reminding me that there are new inventions in medical science every day, and who knows what might be available ten years from now?"

"Exactly." He lowered his hand and sat back.

I shut my eyes and breathed in the fresh scents off the water. "Maybe we should head home," I said. "Diana might want to see Jacob tonight."

We both stood up and I was filled with pleasure when Jesse took my hand.

"I still plan to help you," he said. "I'll try to talk sense into Rick. I'll call him."

The warmth of his hand around mine made my whole body tingle. "I'm happy you want to help me," I said, "even though I don't really understand why."

His eyes smiled at me. "*You don't?* How could you not?"

A wave of pure elation washed over me, and for once I let myself dream of a long and happy future that might be possible after all.

Chapter Forty-three

The following day, I fell asleep on the sofa while Ellen napped. During the nap I had another flying dream.

This was the first time I'd dreamed of flying during daylight hours. It was a unique experience in comparison as I soared over a vast evergreen forest in the rain. Gray thunderclouds hung low in the sky and sharp stinging raindrops pelted my cheeks. My heart began to pound with fear as a gust of wind came out of nowhere and knocked me off balance—if balance was the right word for it. I banked to the right and accidentally flipped over onto my back. I had to kick my legs and struggle to flip back around.

The chill of the foggy air reached my bones, like fingers of death. Soon I began to shiver as I continued to venture forward over unfamiliar territory, so far from home.

I woke in a panic, drenched in sweat, clutching my chest, gasping for air. To my surprise, rain was pelting the window next to me and I felt somewhat reassured. It really had been a dream, nothing more. I'd simply heard the rain against the glass while I slept. There was no need to read anything more into it.

As I rose to my feet, however, I thought about what Jesse had read on the Internet about the meaning of flying dreams and it made sense that I'd had a more frightening experience this time. Because of what was happening with Ellen, I no longer felt quite so secure. I'd been on top of things before with my improved health and the joy of watching her grow, but now my happy life was threatened. It felt like I was no longer in complete control of my destiny.

No wonder the wind flipped me over. It was probably a sign of things to come. A Rick-storm on the horizon.

Ellen began to cry so I went upstairs to change her diaper. I was in the middle of the task, reaching for a wipe when the phone began to ring. I had no choice but to ignore it. Hopefully, whoever was calling would leave a message or call back later if it was important.

Chapter Forty-four

Jesse

I couldn't remember the last time I'd flown in weather as bad as that. The rain was relentless, showering the helicopter windshield like spray from a fire hose. The wind also didn't help matters any. As my co-pilot and I flew higher up the ridge toward the cabin—which we hoped would be visible in the fog—I felt the engine shudder beneath my grip on the cyclic stick.

Before long we spotted the hunter who had fallen into a ravine not far from the cabin. We hovered dangerously low while lowering a basket to retrieve him. Both his legs were broken and we weren't sure about his spine. It was dicey, but the medics secured him on a board and we delivered him safely to the hospital.

Afterward my co-pilot and I flew over the city, back to the hangar where I filled out my report. There were no more calls before the end of my shift and I was thankful because it felt like one of those days—the kind when you begin to question how long your luck will hold out before it takes a sharp turn south.

When I arrived home the first thing I wanted to do was call Nadia, just to hear her voice, but I'd promised her I would call Rick today. I wanted to do that for her first. So I made a pot of coffee to help draw the chill out of my bones. Then I dug my brother's number out of my wallet.

There were a number of reasons why I felt sick to my stomach when I dialed the number and listened to it ring once...twice... then three times in my ear.

I hadn't spoken to Rick in a decade. The last time we spoke I may have broken his nose. He'd since had cancer. And now he was trying to take a child away from her mother.

Just before the fourth ring someone picked up on the other end. "Hello?"

It was a woman.

The fiancée most likely.

She sounded young.

"Is Rick there?" I asked.

"Yes, just a moment." She sounded overly cheerful, like a character out of *The Sound of Music,* singing about her favorite things.

I braced myself for the deep timbre of Rick's voice, which I hadn't heard since the day we fought like a couple of mangy dogs in his musty LA apartment.

"Hello?"

My fists clenched. "Rick? It's Jesse."

There was a long pause and I heard the creak and click of a door closing. "Hi," he said. "Mom told me you might call."

I sat down. "Yeah. She was surprised to hear from me."

"I'm surprised, too," Rick said. "But I'm glad. It's good to hear your voice, Jesse. I mean that."

He sounded nothing like his old self. First of all, the Rick I remembered would never say anything so generous and sentimental to me. There was also a shaky quality in his voice that I'd never heard before. Was he actually torn up?

"It's good to hear your voice, too." It seemed the right thing to say.

"So I guess Mom told you about my cancer scare," he said.

"Yeah. I was sorry to hear about that. You're doing okay now though?"

"I'm doing really well," he replied. "Actually, better than ever. That may sound crazy to you—to anyone who hasn't gone through what I have—but when something like this happens to you, sometimes you're almost grateful for it. It opens your eyes… You know."

My stomach dropped because those were the exact words Nadia had spoken when we sat on the bench by the river.

Suddenly I felt like an outsider to this experience they shared—an experience I knew nothing about.

Well, maybe not nothing. In my line of work, I saw things on a daily basis that most people never see.

But still, I felt a twinge of jealousy to think that Rick and Nadia had a mutual understanding of something so profound.

"I'm glad you're okay," I said. "And I hear you left your job?"

"Yeah. I know it sounds cliché, but I had to get out of that LA rat race. I had enough money put aside in investments and Christine wanted to settle close to her parents, so I sold the condo. Did Mom tell you about Christine?"

"She mentioned her," I said. "Congratulations."

"Thanks. She's an amazing woman. I hope you can meet her sometime."

"That would be nice," I replied—again, because it was the right thing to say. "Listen, the real reason I'm calling…" I raked my fingers through my hair. "I need to talk to you about your daughter."

"You mean Ellen?" He was quiet for a moment. "Mom dropped a lot of bombs on you, didn't she?"

I tapped a finger on my knee and wondered how I was going broach this topic. Looking back on it, I suppose I could have pumped him for information and gotten him to tell me all sorts of things he might not have said otherwise, but I couldn't bring myself to set him up like that. Despite everything, he was still my brother.

"About that..." I said. "When I called Mom and Dad, I already knew you were suing the mother for custody. It's why I'm calling you now."

"How did you know about it?" Rick asked.

Rising to my feet, I moved into the kitchen and leaned against the counter. "Because I met Nadia Carmichael and her sister Diana here in Boston. They told me."

The coffee pot gurgled noisily behind me.

"How the hell did that happen?" Rick asked. "Did they hunt you down? Or was it a coincidence?"

"It wasn't a coincidence," I told him. "I got a phone call from Diana. Somehow she knew I was your brother and that I lived here. She wanted to ask me some questions."

"What did she ask you? And what did you tell her?" The shakiness in his voice had disappeared. He now sounded exactly like the Rick I remembered.

Aggressive. Defensive. Determined to win.

"She and Nadia wanted to know why you changed your mind about not wanting to be involved in Ellen's life. I told them I couldn't answer that because I hadn't talked to you in years, but I think I understand it now, after talking to Mom and Dad."

"You don't understand anything," he replied. "You couldn't possibly."

"Why not?"

"Because you haven't been through what I've been through."

"And you learned so much from it," I said with no shortage of sarcasm.

"That's right."

I shook my head at him. "Maybe I don't need to have a terminal illness to know what you didn't know before. Maybe I've always known what it means to care about people."

"I care," Rick said. "That's the whole point of this. I have a daughter and I should be a part of her life."

"I don't disagree with you," I argued, wanting to stay rational about this, "but have you considered the fact that you're going to break a little girl's heart when you take her away from her mother?"

Rick let out a breath. "You're still missing the point. Everyone knows what matters most is what's best for the child and there is no doubt in my mind that Christine and I will be better parents in the long term. I'm not going to get into all the reasons why—we can do that in court—but surely, if you've met Nadia, you know she's a ticking bomb. The fact that she has heart troubles is just the tip of the iceberg. She's also a single mother with no education and a bad history with abusive men. Do you know what kind of upbringing she had? She was raised in foster homes, then had an alcoholic father who walked out on them. She'll be a terrible mother."

It was lucky for Rick he was on the other side of the country, because if we'd been in the same room together I might have broken his nose again.

"None of that was her fault," I said. "And have you stopped to think that maybe she learned a lot from all those hardships? More than you could ever know? When it comes down to it, you don't know anything about Nadia," I said. "You've never seen her with Ellen. You've never even *met* Ellen."

"I know Nadia better than you do," Rick spat. "You only just met her, for pity's sake."

It was true, I hardly knew Nadia and maybe I was foolish to assume that I knew what kind of woman she was deep down.

In the beginning, I thought I knew Angela. I let myself fall in love with her without caution or the smallest hint of vigilance. I remembered how Angela had become a different person when she told me she was moving out west to be with Rick. She'd turned out to be nothing like the girl I thought I knew. I didn't recognize her and I certainly never suspected she was capable of betraying me as she had.

Maybe I was presuming too much about Nadia as well.

But wasn't this just like Rick to make me doubt myself?

"You're wrong about her," I said. "Nadia's a good mother and you'd know that if you could see her with Ellen. I haven't met Christine, but if she's a decent person like you say she is, I'm sure she wouldn't want to separate them."

"I'm Ellen's father," he insisted, "and as her father I will make sure she has a real family with two respectable parents and a stable home. It'll be worse for Ellen later on if she stays with Nadia."

"I disagree," I said, "and I'm asking you to reconsider. Please, Rick. You could ask for joint custody or visitation rights. Let Ellen stay where she is."

Silence. "That's not going to work for us."

I scoffed. "Why not? Is it too inconvenient?"

"Don't be an idiot," Rick said. "Christine and I are going to start a family. A *normal* family without any of the problems Nadia will present. We want Ellen to be a part of that. She'll be happier and far better off in the long run."

"And what about Nadia?" I asked. "Doesn't she matter at all?"

"She needs to recognize that this is for the best. Ellen will have a better life with us. It would be selfish of her not to let us take her."

By now my blood was boiling and I wanted to smash my phone repeatedly on the counter. Instead, I shut my eyes and counted to ten because I liked my phone.

"If you came out here and met your daughter," I said, "you would see that Nadia is what's best for her. Not you."

Neither of us said anything for a long time. My heart pounded thunderously in my ears.

"We're done here," Rick said. "Don't call me again."

Shutting my eyes with defeat, I lowered my phone and ended the call. Then I quickly dialed Nadia's number.

Chapter Forty-five

I wanted to tell Nadia everything about my conversation with Rick, but not over the phone. She didn't answer my call, so I texted and told her I was coming over. A short while later, I was sitting on her sofa while she fetched me a glass of water.

Her sister Diana had gone to a movie and Ellen was upstairs, asleep for the night.

"Rick thinks he's changed because he wants to be a family man," I said, "but I don't believe he's changed at all because he's not thinking of Ellen's happiness. Not really. He's certainly not thinking of yours. I know my brother, and he's only thinking of what he wants for himself. He's putting a mask on the whole situation by saying it's what's best for Ellen."

Nadia handed me the glass of water and sat down beside me. "Did you ask him if he would consider shared custody?"

"Yes, but he was like a brick wall. He said no."

"And he knows about my health risks," she said. "He plans to use that against me?"

I saw the heartbreak in her eyes and wished there was something I could do to ease her pain. "I'm sorry. I'm mortified."

"Why would *you* be mortified?" she asked, frowning with bewilderment.

"Because he's my brother and I couldn't make the smallest dent in his opinion. *God!* I'm fit to be tied. It takes me right back to how things were ten years ago when I couldn't believe the things he said and did. I tried to talk sense into him then but it made no difference. He just wasn't capable of recognizing someone else's pain." I set the glass of water down on the coffee table and pressed my forehead into the heels of my hands.

Nadia rubbed a hand over my back and squeezed my shoulder. The rapid beat of my pulse slowed down and the fire in my blood began to cool.

"This isn't your fault," she said. "I appreciate that you tried, but he is who he is. I'm glad I know because at least I'll be prepared for what he plans to bring to the courtroom. I'll bring the same thing. If he wants to accuse me of being a bad mother, I'll shine a very bright light on the fact that he wants to destroy a little girl's relationship with her mother. I'll make sure the judge knows how much Ellen and I love each other, and how happy she is here with me and Diana."

I sat back and tried to see clearly through my rage. "You don't deserve this."

"Sometimes bad things happen to good people. I don't think anyone deserves half of what gets thrown at them in life. Not even Rick. He had a rough year, too. It's no wonder he's feeling desperate."

"You're far more understanding than I am."

She reached for my hand. "If there's one thing I learned when I was in the hospital—it's that life is short and we can't waste precious time feeling hateful or carrying grudges. I love Ellen more than anything and I have to believe that it will all work out somehow. That the love I feel for her will win out over whatever Rick is trying to do. And I don't plan on dying anytime soon. I have a new heart and I'm getting stronger every day. Surely this gift came to me for some greater purpose and I believe that purpose is Ellen. I was put on this earth to be her mother. She's the reason I found the strength to live. It couldn't have been for nothing. It couldn't have been a false dream. And if she's meant to be with her father, to know him, then so be it. I just hope he'll see that she would better off being loved by *all* of us."

Whatever doubts I'd entertained about the true motivations behind my attraction to this woman vanished in that instant when I recognized the depth of her wisdom. I was not here because I wanted to fix what I couldn't fix before. I didn't want to save Nadia to make myself feel better because I was unable to save Angela. Nadia was nothing like Angela. She didn't need saving. In fact I felt humbled sitting there beside her. I was in awe. She was all heart from head to foot, and if anything, I was beginning to believe she had come into my life to save *me*.

"I want to be with you," I said without thinking.

"I want to be with you too," she whispered in return.

For a long time we held each other. Then finally, I kissed her.

Chapter Forty-six

Nadia

When Jesse Fraser kissed me on the sofa that night it confirmed my belief in dreams coming true—but I had no idea how relevant that concept would become as we continued to share things with each other.

"Nothing about this day has been easy," Jesse said as he cupped my cheek with his hand, "until now."

"You think I'm easy, do you?" My smirk brought him closer for another kiss that caused my insides to jangle with excitement.

Later he wrapped his arm around me and I rested my cheek on his shoulder.

"That phone call wasn't exactly a walk in the park," he said, "and it was a rough day at work."

"Why? What happened?" I lifted my head to look up at him.

He entwined his fingers around mine, then told me about the hunter who fell into a ravine and broke both his legs. "I wasn't sure if we'd even be able to locate him," Jesse said. "The rain was pelting the windshield and the fog was as thick as soup. At one point, I thought for sure the wind was going to flip us over and drop us into the trees."

My head drew back. "What time was that?"

He thought about it. "I don't know. Sometime between two and three, I guess."

A fire began to burn in my belly as I stared at Jesse. "That's really weird because I had another flying dream today, and it was the first time I ever had one of those dreams during the day. I was taking a nap right here on the couch and I dreamed I was flying over a forest in the rain. It was stressful, not like the other times when I was flying at night."

Jesse sat up. "That is weird."

Our eyes locked on each other's and my heart began to race.

"What's it like when you fly at night?" I asked, though it wasn't an innocent question. I was fishing for information, exploring what was surely a bizarre and preposterous theory. Was I astral projecting in my dreams to wherever Jesse was?

No, that couldn't be true. It was crazy. They were just dreams.

Clearly, I was still a skeptic.

"If I'm flying over the city," he replied, "it's usually pretty calm. There's not as much wind at night."

"You must fly over the hospitals," I said. "You deliver patients, right? You land on the rooftops."

"All the time."

My breaths were coming faster and I sensed by the flash of light in Jesse's eyes that he was thinking the same thing I was.

But he wasn't. He was thinking of something else entirely. Something far more incredible.

Chapter Forty-seven

"When did you have your transplant?" Jesse asked me. "What was the exact date?"

I told him the date and he reached into his pocket for his phone. He stood up and searched for a number. "Excuse me for one second."

He left me there on the sofa while he went into the kitchen to call someone. I tugged at my shirt to straighten it and shifted to a more comfortable position while I waited.

A few minutes later he appeared in the doorway looking white as a sheet. He stared at the phone briefly, then set it down on the coffee table.

"You're not going to believe this," he said.

I blinked up at him curiously. "Believe what?"

He came to sit beside me again and took both my hands in his. "I think I delivered your heart to you."

Chapter Forty-eight

I wasn't quite able to comprehend what he was telling me. "That's impossible."

"Why? I just called my supervisor. I asked him to check the schedule and reports for the day you had your surgery, and I was flying that day. It was all there in the report and I remember it now. I landed at Boston Mass to pick up a medical team and flew them to another hospital to retrieve a donor heart. I can't tell you which hospital…That's supposed to be confidential. But afterward I flew the team back to Boston Mass. How many donor hearts could have been delivered to Boston Mass that day? Not more than one, surely."

Though this was unbelievable to me, I was still fixated on another piece of this puzzle. "You must land on that helicopter pad all the time," I said, "and you work mostly night shifts, don't you?"

He nodded.

"I didn't tell you this," I said, "but over the past few months, every time I had one of those flying dreams, I thought I was dreaming about my donor. I thought maybe I was somehow remembering how his spirit floated out of the hospital when he passed. I know that sounds nuts, but the dreams were so vivid and real, and when I recognized the hospital here in Boston, I was kind of freaked out. Now I'm wondering if I was dreaming about *you.* If I was somehow there with you when you were flying those nights?"

He took hold of my hand. "I don't know about that, Nadia—and I'll be honest, it does seem nuts—but I do know that I picked up a heart on the day you had your surgery and I flew it to the hospital where you were waiting for it."

His gaze dipped lower to my chest.

I was no longer self-conscious around Jesse. Reaching down, I unbuttoned the top three buttons of my blouse, opened my collar and showed him the top of my scar. "Thank you for that."

Our eyes met, he smiled and I was filled with the most breathtaking swell of joy.

"You're more than welcome," he said.

Chapter Forty-nine

Six weeks later

The thirty-day notice to appear in court arrived when I was just heading out for a long walk with Ellen. Seeing the words printed on the page was like a knife in my heart, but I refused to let it defeat me. Instead I focused on the factors that stood in my favor.

I'd had my parental evaluation. It had gone well. Ellen was happy and smiling the entire time, the house was clean and well organized for a growing toddler, and Diana and Jacob had been there to meet the evaluator as well.

It didn't hurt that my sister was a successful attorney engaged to a cardiac surgeon who lived a block away. They made me look good and the evaluator was duly impressed.

On top of that the letter from my doctor made me out to be a transplant superstar. My pathology reports were excellent, my diet and exercise routine superb and all my regular cardiac biopsies over the past six months had showed no signs of organ rejection.

Today, however, as I stood in the blinding sunshine with Ellen strapped into her stroller, I had to accept that despite all those triumphs, I was still required to face Rick in a courtroom and defend myself as a mother.

And I might lose my daughter.

I realized I was now facing a different kind of threat, but no less vital. Just over a year ago I survived heart failure. Now I had to fight to keep my daughter, and that was a life or death situation as well, because if I lost Ellen, how could I possibly go on?

Determined to maintain a positive outlook, I texted Jesse and told him about the notice, then I stuffed it into my bag. As I withdrew my hand, I noticed some redness on my forearm. Was it some kind of rash?

Under normal circumstances I would have called Dr. Reynolds and arranged to have him look at it immediately because I was at high risk for infections that could become life threatening if left untreated. But this wasn't the best time to introduce something dodgy into my medical reports, so I decided to keep a close eye on it and hold off making an appointment for now.

Jesse received my text and called later to ask if I was free for dinner.

"Don't worry about the court date," he said. "Everything's going to be fine. And I have something I want to show you. I just called Diana to see if she was free to watch Ellen for us tonight. She said yes."

"It sounds like an offer I can't refuse," I replied.

He picked me up at five and when I asked where we were going to eat, he told me he'd cooked something for us. It was packed in a cooler in the trunk.

"Although 'cooked' might be a bit of an exaggeration," he added. "I hope you like cold chicken salad. I also stuck a bottle of red wine in there. You're allowed to have red wine, right?"

"In moderation, yes," I replied, wondering what he had in mind for us tonight, because he'd never done anything like this before.

We drove out of the city and headed along the Charles River toward Waltham. Eventually we turned onto a private wooded lane and drove a short distance through lush green foliage.

"Where are we going?" I asked.

"To see a house," he finally explained. "I'm thinking about buying it and I'd like your opinion."

My eyebrows rose. "Really? I thought you liked living in the city."

"I do, but I'm not crazy about my apartment. It's kind of small. Besides, this isn't that far out. It's only a twenty-five minute drive, and there's a hospital in Waltham."

What can I say? I was a woman in love and my hopes were stirred into a frenzy as I imagined that he might have invited me here to talk about long-term plans for us. Together as a couple.

As a family.

Ellen loved Jesse, and so did I. He was the kindest, most generous man I'd ever known, and every time I looked at him I felt like I might swoon. There was just something in his eyes that moved me. Each day since we met, my purpose in life—the reason I received this gift from my donor—became clearer. It was to be happy, fulfilled and to shower my joy upon Ellen and Jesse. I'd felt joyful before Jesse came along, but now that had quadrupled.

The sun was just setting when we reached the end of the narrow lane and the house came into view. It was blue with white trim, surrounded by fertile greenery and overlooked a narrow section of the river.

We pulled to a halt on the gravel driveway and Jesse turned off the car. "There's no for sale sign," I said.

"Not yet," he replied. "I know the guy who's selling and he plans to put it on the market next week. I convinced him to let me take a look first." Jesse reached into his pocket, withdrew a set of keys and dangled them in the air. "Ready?"

"Yeah."

We got out of the car and walked hand in hand to the covered veranda.

"How old is it?"

"It was built around 1910 but it was renovated recently. Doug says it has a new kitchen and bathroom and they replaced the roof two years ago."

"I love the veranda," I said as we climbed the steps. "And look, there's a porch swing." I hurried to sit on it.

Jesse followed but didn't sit down. He leaned a shoulder against one of the square white columns and smiled. "You look perfect sitting there." He dug out his phone and took my picture.

"It's so peaceful here," I said, rising to my feet. "Close your eyes and listen."

We both stood on the porch with our eyes closed, taking in the hush of the forest. Then a chipmunk called from somewhere in the treetops and we opened our eyes.

"Rabble rouser," Jesse said.

"Yes," I replied. "You'll have to lay down the law if you buy this place. Chipmunks must keep it down to a dull roar."

He kissed me on the cheek and led me to the front door. After slipping the key into the lock, he pushed it open and gestured for me to enter. "Ladies first."

I walked in and discovered that the house was completely empty of furniture. There weren't even pictures on the walls.

The floors were hardwood and looked like they could be refinished. Cherry wood paneling covered the walls in the living and dining rooms, and the stair rail was cherry as well.

"It's very beautiful…Kind of has a craftsman style. How long has it been empty?"

"Only a few days," Jesse said. "It belonged to Doug's parents and on a whim they decided to pack up and move down to their condo in Florida." Jesse followed me into the main room where he seemed more interested in looking at me than inspecting the house. "They lived here all their lives," he added, "since they were first married fifty years ago. Lots of love in this house, Doug says."

"I can sense that." I met his gaze with a smile, then I glanced up at the white-painted ceiling to admire a center medallion and wrought iron hanging light fixture. I looked over the wood-burning fireplace and mantel as well. "Where's the kitchen?"

"Through here."

I had the distinct impression, as Jesse gestured toward a door, that he had already been here to see the place on his own.

I followed him into a modern kitchen with cream-colored cabinets and a speckled granite countertop. A large window overlooked the river in the backyard.

"Do the appliances stay?" I asked, admiring the stainless steel fridge and gas range.

"Yes, everything you see is included."

"Even the curtains? They look new. I really like them."

I moved across the breakfast nook, opened a new sliding glass door and walked out onto the back porch. There was a small blue boathouse at the river's edge and some Adirondack chairs on the lawn.

Jesse followed and we both gazed out at the river. "Quite the view, isn't it?" he said.

The water was shiny and calm. I breathed in the fresh clean fragrances of early autumn.

"Do you like this house?" he asked.

"I love it. It's like a dream."

There were times I wondered if I truly *was* dreaming all of this. How could my life have become so miraculous every day when I'd always been the unluckiest woman on the planet?

Or maybe I died during my transplant surgery and went to heaven, and this was it.

But no…Surely God wouldn't let Rick sue me for custody in heaven.

Jesse reached for my hand. "I'm glad you like it because I want to buy it for you. For *us,* I should say. Ellen, too."

My heart was pounding like a jackhammer and I turned to face him. "What are you saying, Jesse?"

"I'm saying that I want to marry you. I want to take care of you and Ellen."

Though I was thrilled to hear him utter those words—*I want to marry you*—together in a sentence, there was a part of me that couldn't help being hesitant and cautious.

I inclined my head at him. "Take care of us…That sounds lovely and I'm flattered, but I don't think that's a good reason to marry someone—so that you can take care of them. I'm in love with you but I don't want you to think I need to be taken care of."

He bowed his head. "Oh, God, I'm sorry. That came out all wrong. Not like I planned it at all, and I don't think that way about you." His eyes lifted to meet mine as he reached into his jacket pocket. He pulled out a small velvet box. I blinked down at it in shock.

"I love you," he said. "I respect and admire you and I want to spend the rest of my life with you." He opened the box and showed me a diamond ring that took my breath away. "Will you marry me?"

Chapter Fifty

I hesitated, perhaps for too long, because Jesse carefully closed the box and lowered it to his side.

I let out a sigh. "I'm sorry. I think we need to talk about this."

He nodded and pointed toward the water. "Let's go sit in those chairs down there."

There were four painted Adirondack chairs facing the river. We crossed the lawn and I sat in the purple one. Jesse took hold of my hand.

"I proposed," he said, "because I love being with you and Ellen and I don't ever want to lose you."

"I believe you," I replied. "We love being with you, too, but does this have anything to do with Rick? Are you just doing this to try and help me win the custody case? Or to prevent Rick from winning it?" It had never occurred to me before that our relationship might be rooted in the bitter competition that existed between these two brothers. I'd never let myself imagine that Jesse might be using me toward that end—unconsciously of course. I didn't believe he could ever be a manipulator, but he might not be sure of his true feelings.

He sat back in his chair. "You know me better than anyone. You know how I feel about Rick, and yes—all of this does take me back to what happened ten years ago with Angela. So I won't lie to you. I'll freely admit that I want to keep you and Ellen safe and make sure he doesn't destroy your life. I want to help you and I'm certain you'll have a better chance in court if he can't wave that single mother argument around. He won't be able to say that he can provide a more stable homelife for Ellen if you and I are married."

"That may be true," I argued, "and I'd be a fool to refuse you if it meant I could keep Ellen—because I'd do just about anything to make sure I didn't lose her. But I don't want you to ever feel like you sacrificed your own future by marrying me. I can't ask you to do that."

He sat forward and spoke with an intensity that caused my blood to race through my veins. "How could you ever think it would be a sacrifice? I fell in love with you the first moment I saw you, and every moment since has been better than the last. You *know* that, Nadia. You also know it would have come to this eventually, with or without the court case. I was never going to let you go or move on. You're it for me and I can't imagine living without you. I'll be honest with you now because I respect you." He took a breath. "You're right. I probably wouldn't have proposed today if Rick wasn't breathing down your neck with his custody suit. I would have waited a little longer because…" He paused. "Well, just because. But since I knew I was going to propose anyway, I figured…why not do it now and help you—*help us both*—keep Ellen?"

I felt breathless. I wanted to run and jump. "Are you sure about this, Jesse?"

"Of course I'm sure." He squeezed both my hands. "I want to marry you as soon as we can arrange it and I want to buy this house and move in right away and build a swing set right over there for Ellen." He kissed the backs of both my hands. "I want to start our life together. I want to go to bed with you every night and wake up beside you every morning. I don't want to waste another minute living apart."

Laughter bubbled up inside me and my eyes filled with tears. "I want that, too," I said. "Let's do it."

He smiled, then rose from the chair and got down on one knee in front of me. "Then let me do this better. Thank God for second chances." He presented the ring to me again and said, "Nadia Carmichael, will you make me the happiest man alive and be my wife?"

I cupped his face in both my hands and kissed him. "Yes. I will."

Then he slipped the ring on my finger and I wondered if I should pinch myself.

Chapter Fifty-one

Jesse and I were married at the courthouse five days later which gave me just enough time to buy a dress, choose some flowers and arrange a small dinner party at a downtown restaurant for our guests, which included Ellen, Diana and Jacob, her parents and her sister, Becky. Her brother Adam wasn't able to attend because he lived in Australia, but he sent us a lovely antique clock for the new house.

Under the circumstances, Jesse chose not to invite his parents or Rick, though I suggested it might be a good way to mend some fences. He said he would think about that in time, but he didn't want anything to spoil our wedding day.

As it turned out, I don't believe anything could have spoiled it. It was a day filled with happiness, hope and blessings. We spent our wedding night at a nearby historic inn which was the extent of our honeymoon for the time being, though we planned to travel somewhere in the spring.

A week later, we took possession of the blue house on the river and Jesse hired movers to take care of everything while I tried not to get worked up about my upcoming court date.

Thankfully the rash I'd noticed on my arm a few weeks earlier disappeared after a day or two and no other health issues arose to upset my wedding plans or the relocation to the new house. I continued to take all my medications and found a moderately strenuous walking trail not far from the house that led to a nearby playground—perfect for Ellen and me.

I was busy the week of our move, unpacking boxes and organizing the kitchen while Jesse worked nights. It was exhausting but exciting and I probably tried to do more than I should have.

"Are you feeling okay?" Jesse asked when we sat down to eat dinner, just the three of us. "You look tired. Your color's not great."

"I *am* tired," I replied as I fastened Ellen's bib behind her neck, "but it's the good kind. I haven't been this busy since before I got sick and it's nice to feel normal again." I took a seat. "If someone had told me when they were wheeling me in for my surgery that a year later I'd be a married woman, I never would have believed it." I gave Jesse a cheeky look. "And my word, this has introduced all sorts of new and exciting "activities" into my daily routine."

He pointed a finger at me. "Behave. There's a child present. But seriously, you should still be careful. Why don't we take it easy tonight? Those boxes can wait."

"All right." I passed the green beans to him. "Want to watch a movie later?"

"Sounds like a plan."

~

The sun shone brightly the following day, so I applied some sunscreen and took Ellen to the playground where we met some other young mothers from the neighborhood. Their children were about the same age as Ellen, which gave us lots to talk about. They shared all sorts of helpful information about activities for families in Waltham. We exchanged phone numbers and I returned home feeling confident that Jesse and I had made the right decision in buying this house and moving out of the city. Everything about the area seemed to fit with the person I had become.

Ellen fell asleep in the stroller on the way home. I didn't want to wake her, nor did I want to leave her in the yard because there were things I wanted to do inside. I knew I couldn't keep an eye on her from the kitchen, so I carried the stroller up the steps with her in it.

When I reached the top, I set her down and had some trouble catching my breath. I couldn't seem to get enough air into my lungs and the all-too-familiar sensation sent me into a panic. My heart began to race and I had to sit down on the porch swing.

I leaned forward, laid a hand over my heart and whispered, "Please God, don't do this to me now."

I had to be in court in five days. Healthy. At the top of my game.

Oh, what had I been thinking? I shouldn't have carried the heavy stroller up the steps. I could have simply parked Ellen in the shade, set the brake and left her there until she woke up. I could have sat here on the swing with a book.

I felt the urge to cough, and once it started, I couldn't stop. Quickly, I checked beneath the hem of my loose-fitting jeans to examine my legs and ankles—because that was one of the symptoms I'd experienced during heart failure. Fluid had gathered in my lungs and caused my legs to swell.

My body looked fine below the knees and eventually the cough settled, but my anxiety level remained high. I was overcome by a terrifying sense of doom. All the questions that had consumed me during my illness and recovery came hurling back to my mind.

Why was this happening? What had I done to deserve it? Was the Grim Reaper obsessed with me? Was his nose out of joint because the surgeons at Mass General had sent him packing? Was he now following me in the shadows, waiting for his chance?

Worst of all I began to ponder the possibility that I might not live as long as everyone expected. This could be it for me. Maybe that's why I was given this new heart and a second chance at life—so that I could be with Jesse and know what it felt like to be part of a real loving family, however briefly it lasted. Maybe this was to be my last hurrah.

I shut my eyes and leaned back on the porch swing. Under any other circumstance, I would have called Dr. Reynolds immediately, but my court appearance was in five days. My medical records had to show that my prognosis was good. Now was not the time for my body to start rejecting this new heart.

Chapter Fifty-two

"I can't believe how much I miss you," Diana said when she popped by that evening to drop off an extra bedside table. She said she didn't need it, which worked out well for Jesse and me because we only had one. At the present moment we were sharing a reading lamp that clipped onto the headboard.

"I miss you, too," I replied, holding the door open for her.

Though I was tempted to take the table out of her hands, I forced myself to back out of her way instead. "You can set it down here. Jesse will take it upstairs when he gets home."

"No, no," Diana replied. "I'll take it up." She plowed ahead to the staircase.

Ellen was toddling around the living room, getting into things as usual. I couldn't leave her, but I couldn't carry her up the stairs either because I was trying not to exert myself, so I scooped her up and settled her in the activity center where I knew she'd be safe. She must have been tired because she didn't object or throw a tantrum.

I followed Diana up the stairs to my bedroom. She carried the table around the foot of the bed and set it down by the window.

"The place looks great," she said as she straightened and pushed her hair away from her face. "It's gorgeous. Though you could use a new bedspread. This came from Jesse's apartment?"

She looked to me for an answer.

"Yeah, what can I say? He's a guy."

She ran a hand over the navy blue fabric. "You should have something natural to sleep under. A hundred percent cotton is nice."

"I'll look for something," I replied.

I showed her what I'd done to the upstairs bathroom and she loved the new shower curtain. She asked where I got it and I told her about a cute little boutique here in Waltham.

"Let me know if you want to have a painting party," she said. "Jacob and I could come over to help."

"We may take you up on that…after we get through next week."

Naturally I was referring to the court date, but I didn't need to explain that to Diana.

We returned to the living room where we found Ellen happily studying her fingers.

"Want some tea?" I asked Diana.

"Sure."

We moved into the kitchen and I plugged in the kettle.

"How are you holding up?" she asked as she took a seat at the table.

"Fine. Trying to stay positive." I opened the cupboard to search for the green tea she liked best, but when I carried it to the table I stopped in my tracks because I saw the way she was looking at me. It wasn't good.

"What's wrong? Do I have something on my face?"

She frowned at me. "No, but something's not right. Are you feeling okay?"

A hot ball of panic exploded in my belly. "I'm fine."

"No you're not, and I can tell when you're lying to me. Are you sure you're okay?"

I rolled my eyes. "Honestly, I'm just worn out from the move."

I set the box of tea on the table and turned to fetch two mugs.

"When's your next appointment with Dr. Reynolds?" she asked.

"I don't know...Next month sometime." I opened the cupboard door and stood on my tiptoes to reach the second shelf.

Then I heard the sound of the chair legs scraping across the floor behind me and braced myself for more questions as I turned to face my twin.

Her palm landed on my forehead. "You don't have a fever," she said. "No other symptoms?"

"None," I replied.

"You'd tell me if there were."

"Of course."

Squinting doubtfully at me, she returned to her chair and sat down. "Okay then. Let's talk about the court appearance. What do you plan to wear? I know it shouldn't matter, but it does."

By now the kettle was boiling. I unplugged it and poured hot water into two mugs—and was grateful for the change of subject.

Chapter Fifty-three

Over the next few days, my inability to climb a flight of stairs without becoming winded continued to concern me—but on the upside, it didn't get any worse. Nevertheless I was careful not to overexert myself. I avoided any strenuous walks with Ellen until I could see my doctor; I got plenty of rest and I tried not to foster undue anxieties about the court date.

That was perhaps the most challenging component—but also the most important because it was crucial that I stay strong and mentally positive about the outcome.

I also had to be realistic.

When Diana came over to deliver the bedside table she prepared me for the most probable result of the custody case—that no judge in his right mind would deny Rick his rights as a father. Rick would be awarded custody, but at the same time, it was unlikely he would receive *full* custody. I was still Ellen's mother and I was a darn good one. Of that, we were both confident.

All the same, in the days leading up to Thursday, I had to resign myself to the fact that Rick, Christine, Jesse and I would be linked together forever as a family. Thanksgivings, Christmases, graduations and weddings…We would have to find a way to get along and I would have to share my precious daughter with others. After Thursday, she would no longer belong only to me. I would be required to consult Rick about many things, as he would be required to consult me.

The night before the case came up in court, as I sat down for dinner with Jesse, I knew it was time to discuss what the future might hold.

"I've made up my mind about something," I said, "and I hope you'll understand because what I want most is for this to go as smoothly as possible."

"That's what I want, too," he replied, passing me the salad bowl.

Our eyes met across the table and I sensed he was referring to tomorrow's events while I wanted to talk about the rest of our lives.

Spooning some cucumbers and cherry tomatoes onto my plate, I soldiered on. "We both know that Rick will likely win some rights tomorrow, and if that happens, I'll want to forge a new relationship with him and Christine. I know we've both been burned by him, but I think it would be best if we try to move past that."

Jesse set down his fork and stared at his plate. "I hope he doesn't win anything, but if he does I'll do my best." Jesse's eyes lifted. "And I'll be doing it for you and for Ellen. Not for him."

"Thank you," I replied, though it wasn't exactly what I wanted to hear.

What I really wanted was to enter this new chapter of my life with a positive outlook and assume the best, not the worst. I wanted to give Rick the benefit of the doubt.

Given the circumstances, I had to believe there was some good in him…There must have been something that drew me in. Certainly, I'd made my share of foolish mistakes when it came to the men in my life, but there had to have been at least *something* sensible in our brief relationship. Something that was meant to be.

I also believed Rick and I had something in common now, besides Ellen. He, too, had looked death in the eye and survived.

Quietly, in my heart, I remained hopeful that he *had* been changed by that experience, despite what Jesse thought.

I didn't say any of that out loud, however, because I knew Jesse wouldn't enjoy hearing it.

In any case, I was about to see Rick again, in person for the first time since before Ellen was born. Jesse didn't know this, but I fully intended to greet him with a warm smile, shake his hand and congratulate him on his engagement. I—perhaps more than anyone—appreciated the importance of new beginnings and second chances. I wanted to get off on the right foot.

After supper, just before Jesse left for a night shift, he held me tight in the foyer and kissed me. "I'll meet you at the courthouse in the morning," he said, stroking my hair away from my face.

"I love you," I replied.

"I love you, too."

When he opened the door a gust of wind blew into the house. A cold, hard rain came down sideways and the treetops swayed wildly.

"Be careful tonight," I said as I watched him pull his hood up over his head and dash down the stairs to the car. I couldn't imagine flying a helicopter in weather like this.

"Always!" he called out as he got in.

I stood in the open doorway with my arms folded against the chilling damp breeze. Jesse started the engine. The headlights illuminated the dark yard as the wiper blades beat across the windshield.

A moment later, he backed out of the driveway and the red taillights disappeared from view.

Please be safe tonight…

I shut the door and locked it, then went to lift Ellen out of her high chair. "Come with me little monkey. It's time for your bath."

With my hands cupped around her tiny hips to keep her steady, I followed her up the stairs.

When we reached the top, I had to stop and rest. Breathing was difficult.

Chapter Fifty-four

I woke to a terrible nightmare.

Not a nightmare about flying through stormy weather, but a real life ordeal where I couldn't get enough air into my lungs.

Stricken with panic, I sat up in bed and fought to gulp in some oxygen. I coughed and wheezed and felt certain I was dying.

The terror of such a thought paralyzed me. I'd suffered heart failure before and I knew what it felt like. This was the same, only different. I felt more desperate and afraid because there was so much more to lose. A year ago it was just me. Alone. Now I had a beautiful life with Jesse and Ellen—and a court appearance in the morning to determine if I was fit enough to be her mother.

Yet here I sat, unable to breathe, unable to lift Ellen out of her crib if she needed me.

Swinging my legs to the floor and sitting up on the edge of the mattress, I turned on the light and willed myself to breathe deeply and calmly. By some miracle it seemed to help. I slid closer to the bedside table, picked up the phone, and dialed Jesse's number.

After four rings, his voicemail kicked in. I left a quick message. "Jesse, I'm not feeling so good. Please call me as soon as you get this."

Where was he? Not in the air I hoped because the wind and rain had so much force they rattled the windows.

I hung up and called Diana. Thank God she picked up right away. "Hello?"

"Hi, it's me." I was still fighting to breathe normally. "I'm at home and Jesse's at work. I can't reach him and I can't breathe."

"Stay calm," she said. "Did you call 911?"

"Not yet, but I'll do that as soon as we hang up. Can you come over here? Ellen's asleep. I don't know what's going to happen and I need someone to be here just in case."

"I'm on my way," she replied. "I'll be there in twenty minutes."

"Thank you." I hung up and immediately dialed 911. Then I noticed the rash on my arm was back.

Chapter Fifty-five

I have no idea what happened after I spoke to the dispatcher. All I remember is describing my symptoms and giving her my address. She told me help was on the way.

The next thing I knew I was lying flat on my back, a siren was wailing, there was an oxygen mask over my face, and I was bumping along on a gurney, staring up at the roof of an ambulance.

I blinked a few times and struggled to make out what was happening. I didn't even know what day it was.

"Welcome back," the female paramedic said, leaning over me. "You gave us quite a scare."

Maybe it was a common reaction for a heart transplant recipient, but I was keenly focused on the physical organ inside my chest. Was it working okay? I swore I could feel it pumping blood to all my extremities. I could hear the sound of it in my ears.

Surely that was a good sign. Or maybe I was *too* aware of it. Not relaxed enough. I needed to calm down.

"I had a heart transplant," I managed to explain from beneath the oxygen mask.

"We know," the paramedic replied with a smile. "We saw the scar and we've already spoken to Dr. Reynolds. He's on duty tonight and we're taking you to Mass General right now."

"Not Waltham?" I asked.

"No," she replied distractedly as she checked a monitor.

The fogginess in my head began to clear as a new wave of panic washed over me. "Where's my daughter?"

"Your daughter's fine," the paramedic replied.

"Is she here?" I tried to sit up but discovered I was strapped down.

The paramedic leaned over me. "Just try to relax. Everything's going to be fine."

My heart was racing. Surely alarm bells were going to start ringing everywhere!

"Nothing's fine," I told her. "I need to know where my daughter is and I have to be somewhere in the morning. It's important."

"I don't think you'll be going anywhere," the paramedic said with an easy smile, as if I only had plans to take in a sale at Filene's.

"You don't understand," I pleaded. "I can't be sick right now and I need to know where Ellen is."

I tried to pull the oxygen mask off my face, but felt light-headed and passed out before I could say anything more.

Chapter Fifty-six

"Who are you?" I asked incredulously as I pulled my hand from the man's grasp. "Let go of me."

"Don't worry," he gently said. "Just try to relax. Everything's going to be fine."

I was really tired of hearing that. I'd heard it too many times over the past year.

"This can't be happening." I stared pleadingly into his eyes. "I have to be in court tomorrow and I need to be healthy. If there's something wrong with my heart, can't we fix it on Friday? *Please*, for the love of God. I promise I'll come back. I'll be here first thing in the morning, but you can't keep me here, and please don't medicate me. I need to be coherent. What time is it?"

Some mad impulse compelled me to look down at the road beneath me, and I realized I was flying. In a dream state.

"Oh *God*!"

Suddenly I became aware of the wind and rain in my face.

Terrified that I was going to crash like a dive bomber into the ground, I reached for the man's hand. He linked his whole forearm around mine and steadied me.

"Relax," he said, sounding almost amused. "You know how to do this."

Of course I knew. I'd flown many times in my dreams, but lately I'd come to believe Jesse was manning the controls.

"Am I dreaming?" I asked.

"Yes," he replied.

"Where's Jesse?" I asked. "Is he all right? The weather's not good. He shouldn't be flying."

"I'm sorry, I don't know," the stranger said.

"You don't know him?"

Why I thought this man would know my husband or have some knowledge of his whereabouts was a mystery. Clearly I was out of my mind.

"What about Ellen?" I asked next. "The last thing I remember I was calling 911 and she was asleep in her crib. I shouldn't be out here."

"She's fine," the man assured me. "Your sister is with her."

"How do you know that?"

"I just do. Now you need to relax. That's the most important thing."

I frowned at him. "Who are you?"

"Alexander," he said.

I looked him over from head to foot and then the dream ended abruptly. At least I *think* that's where it ended. I couldn't remember anything else.

Chapter
Fifty-seven

I woke to the sound of a heart monitor beeping steadily and the sterile antiseptic scents of the hospital—all so very familiar. My eyes fluttered open. Everything was a blur. The world slowly came into focus.

"Ellen?" I still had no idea where she was or where I was. Then I remembered my dream. Was Diana with her?

"Honey..." Jesse leaned over me and kissed my forehead. "Thank God you're all right."

"Am I?" I wasn't entirely sure if this was real. My head still felt fuzzy. I was groggy and confused. "Is it morning?" I glanced toward the window and saw daylight.

"It's the afternoon, actually," he explained, cupping my cheek in his palm.

I stared up at him with concern. "Did you fly last night? I was so worried."

"No," he replied. "It was a miracle we didn't get any calls."

Pushing the dream from my mind, I struggled to focus on the present. "What about my court appearance? Did I miss it?" The beeps on the heart monitor began to accelerate as my stomach churned with nervous knots. "Please tell me Diana was able to reschedule it."

Just then Diana walked into the room with Ellen in her arms. I let out a sharp breath of relief when I saw my baby.

"Ellen..."

"You're awake," Diana said. "Thank heavens."

Ellen reached out with her pudgy little hand. "Mumma."

"Hi sweetie. I missed you!" It took all the strength I possessed to convey an air of health and happiness when I still found it immensely difficult to breathe, and I was anxious about what had happened to me. *Was I in heart failure again?* I still didn't know. "Come over here and give me a hug."

Diana carried her to my bedside.

Carefully I sat up and was able to wrap my arms around my darling little angel. For a long moment, I held her close and celebrated the fact that my heart, despite all its failings and weaknesses, was swelling with love. It flooded my whole body with warmth and gratitude. I didn't want to let go of Ellen, but I knew I couldn't hug her forever.

"I'm happy to see you," I whispered in her ear and gave her a quick kiss on the cheek. "Why don't you lie down here?" I patted the bed beside me and she snuggled down.

My bed was propped up so I was not lying flat, but I could still feel an uncomfortable pressure on my chest and I wanted to cough.

When Ellen spotted the IV tube sticking out of the back of my hand, she reached for it. I quickly raised my hand over my head.

"We can't touch that," I gently explained. "It's called an IV tube. It feeds me medicine."

"IB toob," she repeated before laying her head back down on my shoulder.

I waited for her to settle down, then I looked up at Jesse and Diana.

"What happened this morning?" I asked them. "Obviously I missed being in court."

Diana turned to Jesse. "Why don't you take Ellen downstairs to the cafeteria for a few minutes?"

"Yeah." He approached the bed, lifted Ellen into his arms and gave me a kiss on the forehead. "I'll be back in a little while." He encouraged Ellen to wave as they walked out. "Say bye to mommy."

None of this was helping my current state of unease.

"Please tell me what's going on," I said to Diana as soon as we were alone.

She sat down in the chair beside the bed and took hold of my hand. "This isn't going to be easy for you to hear. You're going to have to be strong."

"You're scaring me."

"I'm sorry, I don't mean to, but there's no easy way to say this. It didn't go well this morning. The judge refused to reschedule and he based his decision on the fact that you weren't well enough to be there today."

"I don't understand," I said, my eyebrows pulling together as I frowned. "What did he decide?"

Diana squeezed my hand and took a breath. "He awarded full custody to Rick and Christine. You have virtual and supervised visitation rights only."

Her words sank slowly into my consciousness, but my brain shoved them out. "No. That can't be right."

"I'm sorry, Nadia."

I shook my head at her. "No, that can't be what happened. I'm Ellen's mother. They can't just take her away from me."

Diana continued to hold my hand, no doubt giving me time to digest what she had told me.

I lay there in a cloud of disbelief, wondering again if this was a nightmare from which I couldn't wake—a nightmare that began when I caught that virus that destroyed my heart. It just kept going on and on, week after week, month after month.

"I must be cursed," I said. "No one can be this unlucky in a single lifetime."

Though, to be fair, I'd had my share of good luck, too. Especially lately.

But not today.

"I don't understand how that could have happened," I said, "how any judge could be that unfair. And where were you? Where was Bob? Was no one representing me this morning?"

"I was there," Diana replied, "and Bob did everything he could. He fought hard, but none of it mattered. It was almost as if Judge Cassidy had his mind made up before we even got there, and I'm sure the result would have been the same whether you were there or not. I know it's unprofessional for me to say this, but he's an ass. And Rick's lawyer didn't have any official diagnosis about what happened to you last night, but he kept hammering away at the fact that you're vulnerable to illness and this proved it, and that Ellen needs to be in a more stable environment. The judge agreed."

"But surely if I hadn't been sick…" I argued, "if I'd been there on time this morning he would have ruled differently. Don't you think?"

Diana shook her head. "I don't know."

"Did Bob remind the judge that Rick had cancer last year?" I asked. "Did he hammer the fact that Rick wasn't perfectly healthy either?"

"He did," Diana replied, "but the judge congratulated Rick on his recovery."

"What about *my* recovery?" I shouted. "I have a new heart for pity's sake. I went to hell and back."

Diana bowed her head. "I know. You've fought so hard and have come so far. You don't deserve this." We sat quietly for a moment while my thoughts spun through all the logistics.

"Supervised visits?" I said. "Virtual visits? What does that even mean? And will Rick and Christine be allowed to take Ellen to California? When will I be able to see her, and how often?"

Instead of answering my questions, Diana said, "Don't worry, we're going to fight this."

"Don't worry!" I laughed bitterly. "How can I not worry?"

My agitation caused the beat of my heart to accelerate and the fluid in my lungs sent me into a coughing fit.

Diana helped me sit up. A nurse came in to check on me, but I was able to stop coughing on my own and she left.

After all that, I realized I hadn't even asked the question I should have asked as soon as I opened my eyes.

My heart…What was wrong with it? Was this the end?

I lay back on the pillows and stared up at the white ceiling. "Maybe the judge is right," I said. "Maybe it's better this way."

"What are you talking about?" Diana asked reproachfully.

"Maybe it would be best if Ellen didn't get too attached to me. She's so young and what if something happens to me when we're alone? No child should have to lose a mother. Maybe I *am* being selfish. Maybe I should be thankful that Rick is willing to take her."

"Are you insane?" Diana scolded. "Say something like that again and I'll tell the nurse to send you straight to the psych ward."

"But it's true," I said. "If I'm in heart failure again it's only a matter of time before—"

"Stop it right now," Diana said, "because you're not in heart failure, you turkey head."

I blinked a few times. "I'm not?"

"No. Your heart's fine. It's working great. Better than great. You have pneumonia and Dr. Reynolds said it's a fairly mild case. But you were very agitated last night and you fainted after you called 911. That's why they had to sedate you. You just need to rest up and he's going to adjust your medications."

Sitting up, I shook my head. "But I had a rash on my arm…"

"They looked at that too and they think it might be an allergic reaction. They want to know what sunscreen you've been using."

I blinked up at the ceiling. "*Sunscreen…?* I'm not dying?"

"No, you're going to be okay."

I covered my face with my hands. "Well, that's great, but why did this have to happen *now*? Of all nights…"

"It wasn't the best timing," Diana said, "I'll give you that."

I looked up. "When are they supposed to take Ellen?"

Diana bowed her head and sighed. "Oh Lord, Nadia. I wish I could tell you something different, but they'll be picking her up tomorrow morning."

My eyes nearly popped out of my head. "*What*?"

"They're flying back to Sacramento on Sunday."

The fatigue that had plagued me over the past week was swept away on a flood of adrenaline that catapulted me to my feet. I yanked the IV tube out of my hand.

"You shouldn't do that," Diana said, also rising to her feet.

"I can't be here right now," I explained. "I have to find Jesse and go home." I hurried to the closet. "Are my clothes in here?"

"Yes, but you haven't been discharged."

"I'll sign myself out. They can't force me to stay."

While I picked up the bag that contained the pajamas I was wearing when I called 911 last night, I let out a huff of frustration and headed to the bathroom to change.

I could feel Diana wanting to follow me inside. "You're not going to do anything stupid are you?"

"Like what?" I shut the bathroom door in her face.

"Like suddenly decide to take Ellen on an extended vacation to Mexico?"

I rolled my eyes as I stepped into the silk polka dot pajama bottoms and pulled on a pair of socks. "Don't be ridiculous."

I had to stop to cough, then I pulled on the pajama top and fastened the buttons.

"Are you okay?" Diana asked through the door. "What are you planning?"

"I told you, I'm going to find Jesse so that we can take Ellen home." I opened the bathroom door. "Then I'm going to call Rick and do what I should have done ages ago."

"What's that?" she asked.

"Beg."

"It won't make any difference," she said.

"How can you be so sure?" Diana followed me to the bedside stand where I picked up my cell phone and checked the messages.

"Because Jesse already tried talking him out of this," she said, "and it didn't do any good. And I tried calling him too. Not as a lawyer, but as your sister."

I halted in my tracks. "You didn't tell me that."

She shrugged. "I had to try."

"Well," I said, pulling my hair into a ponytail, "I guess that means it's my turn to try. Nothing ventured, nothing gained, right?"

I walked out to the nurses' station and asked to be discharged.

Chapter Fifty-eight

Shortly after we arrived home, Jesse handed me the phone. "Good luck," he said before backing out of the room and closing the bedroom door behind him.

I waited until the sound of his footsteps disappeared down the stairs, then I took a deep breath and dialed Rick's cell phone number. It rang only once.

"Hello?"

I swallowed uneasily. "Hi Rick? It's Nadia."

There was a long pause before he spoke. "Hey there. Geez, how are you doing? I heard you were back in the hospital last night. Are you okay?"

"I am," I replied, relaxing somewhat when I recognized the note of concern in his voice. It took me back to the early days when I first met him, when he was still with Diana. Back then I thought he was the matrimonial catch of the decade…when he'd been so charming. So warm and charismatic. And he'd come to my rescue on more than one occasion. I really believed he cared and that's why I fell for him.

Now I refused to believe that he didn't possess a single shred of humanity. If it was there I was determined to reach it.

"They sent me home this afternoon," I continued. "It wasn't anything too serious. Just a mild case of pneumonia, but obviously bad timing."

"Yeah, I guess so," he said. "I was surprised when you didn't show up this morning, but I'm glad to hear you're okay."

I closed my eyes with relief and inched back to recline on the pillows.

"I'm glad to hear you're okay, too," I said. "I heard about your health issues. I'm sorry you had to go through that. I know what it feels like."

He cleared his throat. "I'm sure you do and I won't lie. It was rough. And hey…I'm sorry I didn't send a card or something when you were sick. I should have come to visit you. I regret that I didn't."

His words were music to my ears. I felt a flutter of hope…

"Please, you don't have to apologize," I replied. "We were in a weird place back then, you and me. But everything changes when you have a brush with death, doesn't it? I find it so much easier not to sweat the little things these days. You realize how important it is just to be happy, to enjoy each moment and live your life the best way you can."

"I know exactly what you mean," he agreed. "I'm not the same guy I was before." He paused. "Sometimes I wish I had a time machine so I could go back and start my life over, knowing what I know now. But that's not possible so I just have to keep moving forward. Try to be a better person." He paused again. "I really hope we can be friends, Nadia."

Oh, thank God. My heart swelled with joy and I rose to my feet. "I'd like that, Rick—very much—because I don't want to lose all the good memories from the time we spent together. You were amazing to me and you helped me so much. Sure, we made some mistakes, but who hasn't? What matters is that you learn from them. It's why I'm calling, actually. I'm sure there must be some way to—"

To my surprise, he cut me off.

"Listen..." he said. "I'm really glad you called and everything and that we had a chance to talk about this stuff, but please don't ask me to change my mind about coming to get Ellen tomorrow because that's not going to happen. I know it's tough for you and I'm sorry, but the judge made his decision today and it's for the best. Surely you know that."

My heart sank and I felt my nails bite into my palms. "No, I don't know that because it's *not* for the best. She's my daughter and I love her."

"Of course you do," he replied. "I understand that and I sympathize. But we have to think about what's best for Ellen and after what happened to you last night, you of all people should know that over the long term she'd be better off with Christine and me."

I clenched my jaw and fought the urge to say a few choice words, words I might regret later. Though what I really wanted to do was grab him by the shoulders and shake him until his teeth fell out.

"She loves me," I said, "and she's happy here. This is her home. If you take her away and don't let her see me, you'll break her heart."

"She's just a baby," he argued, "which is why it's important that we do this now. At this age she won't even remember the life she had with you in Boston. Judge Cassidy agreed with that line of thinking and if *you* were thinking of her welfare, not yours, you'd agree, too. But you're not. You're only thinking of yourself."

"Judge Cassidy agreed because he's an idiot," I firmly stated, then I bit my lip in an effort to check myself. "I'm sorry. Please listen. You know what it was like for me being orphaned at birth and separated from Diana. That's the last thing in the world I want for Ellen and it should be the last thing you want for her, too."

Feeling as if I were plummeting into a deep vat of defeat, I sat down on the bed and began to desperately try to negotiate. "I truly believe that Ellen will be better off if we all raise her together and if she isn't separated from any of us. We can share equal custody. Wouldn't that be better? Ellen would have four parents who love her instead of two."

Rick was quiet for a moment. "You really believe it would be all sunshine and roses with me and Jesse trying to get along raising the same kid? We'd tear each other's throats out."

"She's not just some *kid*," I argued. "She's our daughter and Jesse loves her. He'd do anything for her and that includes getting along with you."

Knowing their history and having this conversation now, I couldn't imagine any greater sacrifice. But he'd do it. I knew he would.

Rick let out a weary sigh. "There's really no point discussing this, Nadia. We're wasting each other's time because I'm not going to change my mind. I'm coming to get Ellen tomorrow and if you want to try and take me to court again, that's your choice, but I hope you'll just let it go because you know it's for the best."

"*Let it go*? You really have no idea what it means to love a child, do you?" I squeezed my eyes shut, made a fist and pressed it to my forehead. "Please let me talk to Christine."

"She's not here."

"Where is she?"

"Gone out," he replied.

I took a deep breath and counted to ten. "Where are you staying?"

"I'm not telling you that," he replied. "And I swear to God, if you try and harass me or Christine you'll lose your visitation privileges altogether. I'll get a restraining order if I have to. Just accept the terms of the arrangement and leave us alone."

I squeezed my eyes shut again. Diana would shoot me if she could hear this conversation. "Please don't hang up," I pleaded.

Click. The line went dead.

A few minutes later, after I wiped the tears from my cheeks and cleaned up the broken box of crayons I'd thrown against the wall, I walked out of my bedroom and returned to the living room.

"You're right," I said to Jesse when I found him sitting on the floor with Ellen, playing with a toy. "He hasn't changed at all."

Jesse stood up, walked toward me and gathered me into his arms.

Chapter Fifty-nine

I can't even begin to describe the moments leading up to Rick's arrival at our door the following morning. It was like facing death all over again—worse, actually.

I wasn't surprised that he chose not to bring Christine. Perhaps there was a part of him that was ashamed and didn't want her to see the emotional horrors that would take place when he took my baby. Or maybe he feared he might end up brawling in the dirt with the estranged brother he hadn't seen in a decade and didn't want Christine to witness that.

Poor Jesse. I knew how difficult it was for him to go outside and teach Rick how to fasten Ellen's safety seat into the rental car. I wasn't sure Jesse could manage it without sneaking in a sucker punch, but he maintained his self-control.

I wrapped Ellen in her blanket and held her on my lap while we watched them from the porch steps.

I, too, had to fight to keep my composure. "That's your daddy," I said, not wanting to cause her any anxiety. "His name is Rick."

"Wick," she repeated.

"That's right, but you can call him Daddy."

"*Daddy.*"

This was something I wasn't sure my new heart could endure.

When they secured the car seat, Jesse came to fetch us. "It's time," he said.

A vein pulsed at his temple. A muscle twitched at his jaw.

"I don't think I can do this," I said shakily.

"We have to," he replied, "but we'll get her back. I promise. I won't rest until we do."

I rose to my feet and carried Ellen to the car where Rick stood waiting. I felt as if I were climbing steps to an executioner's block.

Desperately I glanced to the edge of the yard and wondered how far I could get if I suddenly bolted into the woods. Not far, I knew. Not with these lungs still full of fluid.

"You're doing the right thing," Rick said to me when I reached him.

I wanted to hit him. "But are *you*?" I asked with a scowl.

He didn't flinch. Not even a single spark of doubt or regret flashed in his eyes.

Hearing Jesse's footsteps on the gravel behind me, I forced myself to buckle Ellen into the car seat while struggling to put on a brave face for her. "There we go," I said cheerfully. "All buckled in."

"Buckood in!" she repeated.

I covered her with her blue blanket and turned to Rick. "She likes to hear a story before bed. I put her favorite book in the suitcase. It's called *Hairy Maclary's Caterwaul Caper*. It's about a dog. And her blanket is called Ouwix."

"Thanks," he said.

I had a lump in my throat the size of a kiwi.

I turned to look down at Ellen in the car seat.

Was it true? I wondered. Would she really forget me in time?

She seemed so oblivious to what was happening here. Would she grieve for me as I would grieve for her? Every day for the rest of my life?

I thought of my biological mother who had died on the day I was born. It hadn't been a conscious thing, but I knew I had grieved.

When it was time to shut the car door, I couldn't do it. I began to tremble and Ellen must have picked up on my feelings because she began to cry. Within seconds she was hysterical.

"Please, Rick," I pleaded as he got into the driver's seat. "Don't do this."

But he *did* do it. Without an apology or the smallest show of compassion for our pain, he shut the car door.

Before I could say another word, he was stirring up gravel as he backed out of the yard.

The last thing I saw was Ellen's panic-stricken face in the window and her hand reaching out to me as she cried, "Mummy!"

Chapter Sixty

I barely remember anything about the rest of the day other than the fact that I spent the whole of it, until sundown, curled up in a ball on my bed, staring at the wall. Jesse lay beside me, but I couldn't speak or move. I was numb and inconsolable.

Jesse knew there were no words to fix this, so he didn't try, beyond giving me his solemn vow that we wouldn't give up, no matter how long it took.

Then he simply held me because he understood. I pressed my ear to his chest and listened to the steady beat of his heart.

It was the only thing that soothed me.

Diana arrived at suppertime with a pot of chicken soup and a new plan to try and get Ellen back. I wasn't hungry, but I wanted to hear what she had to say so I dragged myself out of bed and joined her and Jesse at the kitchen table.

As the hour grew late, however, I couldn't focus on legalities because I was worrying about Ellen going to sleep in a strange place with unfamiliar people.

Was she frightened? Was she missing me and Jesse? Was she longing for the sound of my voice? The smell of this house?

I wanted desperately to call Rick and ask if Ellen was all right. I also wanted to talk to the elusive Christine—who was now a spineless coward in my eyes, for not accompanying her future husband that morning to collect her pretty new baby and witness my grief.

Diana talked me out of calling, of course. She didn't want to take the chance that Rick might follow through on his threat to seek a restraining order.

"That won't help our case," she told me.

So I refrained.

It should be mentioned, however, that what surprised me most throughout the ordeal was the fortitude of my new heart. I was able to survive that day so it must have been made of steel.

I didn't dream about flying that night—mostly because I hardly slept a wink. When I did manage to doze off for brief intervals, I dreamt only of Ellen crying for me in the darkness. Then I woke repeatedly in a state of tormented agony and stared at the wall again. In the darkness.

Be strong, my darling baby girl.

Could she hear my thoughts across the distance? I wondered. Would she understand them if she could? I truly didn't know.

Chapter Sixty-one

I must have plunged into a deep, deathlike slumber around dawn because it was past nine o'clock when I my eyes fluttered open.

At first the world seemed normal. Then I remembered what had occurred the day before and a dark cloud of sorrow settled over me. My baby's crib was empty. She was gone.

I sat up in bed, overwhelmingly aware of the silence. Mornings were usually such an active time with Ellen. We laughed and talked and got ready for the day.

It was eerily quiet. I felt like a ghost.

Tossing the covers aside, I rose from bed and stepped into the shower where I sat down on the tiled floor under the hot spray and remained there until the water turned cold. At that point, I stood up and shut off the faucet.

I returned to my room, pulled on a pair of faded blue jeans and T-shirt, but didn't bother to dry my hair or apply makeup before going downstairs.

I found Jesse at the kitchen table reading the paper. Startled by my quiet approach, he jumped when he saw me, set the paper down and looked up at me.

"Good morning," he said. "Are you hungry? I made you an egg-white omelet. Peppers and mushrooms, just the way you like it, and I boiled water for tea."

I stared at him, unable to speak.

He stood up and pulled out a chair for me. I shook myself out of my stupor and sat down.

"You are a true gentleman," I replied. "Thank God I have you."

"And thank God I have you." He pushed my chair in and kissed the top of my head.

How grateful I was for his gentle kindness and understanding. He didn't try to talk me out of my grief. He knew I couldn't possibly pretend it didn't exist.

"How about a grapefruit?" he asked as he picked up the skillet and a spatula. "I ate the other half of one this morning. I could get it—"

"No, that's fine. This is enough."

He slid the omelet onto my plate. "Orange juice?"

"Sure," I replied, just to give him something to do.

He set the skillet back on the stove, poured me a glass of juice and handed me my anti-rejection pills. Then he joined me at the table.

I had to force myself to swallow the first few bites because I had no appetite, but I knew how important it was to keep up my strength and stay healthy. If I was going to see Ellen again, I might have to get on a plane.

Jesse covered my hand with his. "I know this is rough," he said, "but it's going to turn out okay. I have a feeling about it. Rick will come around. Once he gets to know Ellen, he'll understand what she needs."

"If the prospect of his own death couldn't change him," I said, "what makes you think he'll suddenly turn over a new leaf now?"

Jesse bowed his head, for he had no answer.

The sound of a car rolling into the yard caused us both to look up. Jesse slid his chair back and strode to the window.

"It's him," he said. "It's Rick."

I dropped my fork and nearly knocked my chair over as I stood and rushed to the door. "Is Ellen with him?"

"I don't know. I can't tell."

I pushed the door open and dashed out onto the porch. The sun was shining and the light reflected blindingly off the windshield of his car. Shading my eyes with a hand, I hurried down the steps.

Both of the front car doors opened at once and Rick got out of the driver's seat. Over on the passenger side a woman got out and gazed up at the house.

Manners failed me. I ran across the yard and slapped my palms up against the back seat window where Ellen was strapped into her safety seat, clutching her blue blanket, her face beet red from crying.

Without saying hello to Rick or his fiancée, I pulled the door open and sobbed with joy upon seeing Ellen again. "My sweetheart! I'm so happy to see you!"

With frantic, trembling hands I unbuckled her from the seat and lifted her into my arms. *Oh, God...*I can't possibly describe how good it felt to hold her, how my whole body was flooded with an earth-shattering sense of relief and dismay.

She wrapped her legs around my waist and grabbed my neck in a choke hold. "Mummy!"

I wept tears of joy just to have her in my arms, even for a single moment, and dropped to my knees to hold her tight. I cupped the back of her sweet little head in my hand and kissed her repeatedly on the cheek. "I love you so much."

I have no idea what Rick and Christine were doing. They were not even a blip on my radar. The only thing that mattered was Ellen.

When I finally drew back to look at her face, her eyes were bloodshot and her skin blotchy from the stress of crying so hard. I glanced up at Christine, who looked concerned as she stood over me.

I ignored her at first and continued to soothe Ellen. When at last she calmed and her bawling was reduced to frequent hiccups, my own breathing grew slower and I took a moment to collect myself before rising to my feet.

"You must be Christine," I coolly said.

She was not at all what I'd expected. I'd imagined her to be tall and supermodel-gorgeous. The Christine of my imagination wouldn't be caught dead in anything but a short skirt and high heels. She would have silky blonde hair that was straightened twice daily by a professional-grade flat iron, and her nails would be French manicured.

To the contrary, the woman before me was of average height with shoulder-length brown hair and black plastic-rimmed glasses. She had a freckled complexion and wore kaki-colored capri pants with a slightly clashing yellow T-shirt and white sneakers. She was every inch a science geek. Not at all Rick's usual type.

She held out her hand to shake mine. "Hi, Nadia. It's nice to meet you."

Ellen still clutched my neck with a death grip, so I awkwardly shifted her in my arms to shake Christine's hand. "Hi."

Rick approached. "She's certainly happy to see *you*."

I hugged her tight. "I'm happy to see her, too."

The sound of Jesse's voice and his footsteps across the gravel yard caused me to turn. "Did your flight get delayed?" he asked Rick.

"No, it's on time," he replied. "We still have a few hours."

Jesse rested his hands on his jean-clad hips. "Then what are you doing here?"

My gaze darted from one man to the other and I prayed they wouldn't choose this moment to resolve all their differences by duking it out on the lawn.

"We're here because it's the right thing to do," Rick replied.

None of us said anything for a moment.

"I don't understand," I said. *Please don't toy with me. I won't be able to take it.*

"Can we come in?" Rick asked.

Without a word, Jesse gestured toward the front porch.

We all climbed the steps and entered the house. "Have a seat," Jesse said.

But Christine remained standing. "What a lovely home you have." She crossed the living room to the fireplace and examined the framed photographs on the mantle. "Is this your twin sister?" She glanced at me as she picked up the photo.

"Yes, that's Diana," I replied.

Christine set it back down and regarded me sheepishly before moving to the sofa to sit down beside Rick.

With Ellen still clinging to me like a baby chimpanzee, I paced around the living room, bouncing at the knees, hoping the movement would continue to calm her. I wanted her to feel happy again. I wanted to see my baby smile.

"We're here," Christine said, "because we think we made a mistake." She laid a hand on Rick's knee.

Jesse and I exchanged glances.

"What do you mean?" Jesse asked.

Rick cleared his throat. "Ellen cried the whole night. Nothing we did made any difference. She was pretty miserable."

"It broke my heart," Christine added. "I didn't know what to do. I don't have any experience with kids and I hadn't thought it would be like that. We probably should have brought her home to you last night, but I wanted to see if she might settle down. She didn't."

"She didn't sleep at all?" Jesse asked.

"Only a small bit," Christine replied. "It doesn't take a rocket scientist to understand that she's very attached to you, Nadia, and I think she understood that she wasn't going to see you again any time soon."

I hugged Ellen tightly. "I'm attached to her, too."

Christine nudged Rick, as if urging him to contribute something.

"I'm sorry," he said. "I honestly had no idea it would be like that. I wish I could take it all back."

"Take *what* back?" I asked, shooting him a look.

"The court case," he replied. "Our conversation yesterday. I've been a jerk and I should have known it wouldn't be as simple as I thought it would be."

"What are you saying?" Jesse asked.

"I'm saying that I was wrong to take her. She belongs here. It's where she wants to be, and after about six hours of constant crying for 'Mummy' through the night, I knew she wasn't going to just forget you." He was looking at me when he spoke the words and I almost dissolved into a puddle of relief. "If we take her back to California with us today," he continued, "it'll probably scar her for life. And us, too."

Jesse rose from his chair, rushed toward me and Ellen and gathered us both into his arms. We held each other and wept.

"Are you going to leave her here then?" Jesse asked shakily, wiping the tears from his eyes as he turned to face his brother.

Rick nodded. "We talked it over this morning and we think it would best to give you back custody if you want it. But we'd like visitation rights a few times a year and I want her to know I'm her father. If we can reach an agreement, it should move through the system fairly quickly."

I nodded my head. "That would be wonderful. We'd love to have you visit—or if you'd like us to bring Ellen to visit you in Sacramento that would be okay, too. And I'll need to call Diana to arrange everything."

"Of course," Rick said. "We'll let the lawyers work it out."

I met Rick's gaze and held it. "Thank you for bringing her back."

He nodded at me. Then he and Christine stood up.

"We should be going," she said. "We have a plane to catch." They moved around the coffee table and approached me. "Bye-bye, Ellen," Christine said in a cheerful voice as she rubbed Ellen's back. "We'll come back and visit you again, but we'll take it slower next time." As she moved toward the door, Christine addressed me privately. "Maybe the four of us could spend some time together until she feels more comfortable with us."

"I'd like that," I said. "And so would Ellen."

I glanced over my shoulder at Jesse who was following me out. He rolled his eyes, but there was some humor in them.

Outside, the morning sun was warm on my face as we escorted Christine and Rick to their car. By now Ellen was feeling better and was willing to let Rick shake her hand.

"Bye-bye, kiddo," he said. "Hope to see you soon." He turned to Jesse. "Thanks for taking care of her. It helps to know she's in good hands."

Jesse nodded and they regarded each other steadily for a long moment.

"And I'm sorry about a lot of other things..." Rick added, looking down at his shoes. "You're a good man, Jesse. The best I know."

He turned quickly and got into the car.

Jesse slid his hands into his pockets. When Rick started the engine, Jesse stepped forward and rapped a knuckle on the window. Rick pressed the button to lower it.

"Do you know the best way to get out of here?" Jesse asked. "It's quickest if you head back into town, then get onto Newton Street. Left on High Street, right on Cherry, then right again on Washington. That'll get you to the turnpike ramp."

"Thanks," Rick said. He turned to Christine. "Did you get that?"

She smiled. "Yeah, I got it."

Jesse bent forward to speak to Rick in the driver's seat. "And be sure to give us a call when you get home so we know you arrived safely. Here's my number." He reached into his back pocket for his wallet and pulled out his card. "That has my cell number and a number where you can reach me at work. Feel free to call. Anytime. I mean that, Rick."

"Thank you." Rick handed the card to Christine. "You already have mine?"

"Yeah." Jesse gently tapped the roof of the car with his open hand, then took a few steps back to give Rick space to turn the car around. They both waved as they drove off.

Jesse and I stood in silence staring after the car. I think we were both in shock.

"Did that really just happen?" I asked, glancing up at him.

"I think so," he said, holding out his arms to Ellen. "Unless we're dreaming right now."

I passed Ellen across to him and she clutched him around the neck, wrapped her legs around his waist. A lump formed in my throat as I watched him close his eyes and hug her tenderly. "Thank God," he whispered.

He put his arm around me and together we turned and walked back into the house.

Chapter Sixty-two

Five days later I received an email from Christine. I called Jesse over to the computer to read it with me.

"Is she serious?" Jesse asked, leaning forward beside my chair.

"Looks like it. She says they're leaving next month."

Evidently, after talking about it during the flight home, she and Rick had decided to travel to Africa and help build schools in small villages. Christine managed to get a six-month leave of absence from her job.

Jesse pointed at the email. "She says they'll probably adopt at least one child while they're there—maybe two or three if they're siblings—and bring them home to raise here." He straightened and pushed his hair back off his forehead. "I think the world just shifted on its axis."

I chuckled. "I think you're right. It's incredible. She's *really* good for him, you know."

Jesse squeezed my shoulder. I stood up from my chair and pulled him into my arms.

Then *boom*! Ellen toddled into the back of Jesse's knees and said, "Evatoo!"

He looked down at her. "You want to play elevator?"

She giggled. "Evatoo!" Then she picked up her blue blanket and swung it through the air. "Fwying!"

After supper, the three of us snuggled together on the sofa in front of the television. Jesse flipped through the channels and stopped at a nature documentary on PBS.

"Great footage," he said.

The three of us watched aerial shots taken over the ocean from a low-flying helicopter, then the ascent over a rugged coastline where the waves exploded on the rocks.

Ellen pointed her little finger at the screen. "*Ouwix.*"

I gazed down at her, confused. "Do you want your blanket? It's right here." She was already holding it on her lap.

Sleepily, she laid her head on my lap and continued to stare at the television. "*Ouwix.*"

I stared at it, too, mesmerized by the views over a fast flowing river and waterfall.

Abruptly I sat up.

"What is it?" Jessie asked with concern. I could feel his eyes on me.

I shook my head with confusion. "This is just like my flying dreams, and I forgot that I had another one when they took me to the hospital in the ambulance."

I sat forward, still staring at the television, though my mind was somewhere else. "I need to check something."

Gently I shifted Ellen onto Jesse's lap and went to log into the computer.

"What are you looking for?" he asked.

"I want to check obituaries for the day I had my transplant." I typed the question into the Google search field and waited for the results to pop up. "I'm looking for someone named Alexander. Or Alex."

Ouwix.

After a few clicks, an obituary with a photograph appeared.

There he was—the man in my dream who had flown with me to the hospital that night before the scheduled court appearance.

I quickly read over the text and learned that Alexander Fitzgerald was a firefighter in Manchester who had died on duty.

Swiveling around in the chair, I asked Jesse, "Did you bring my heart from Manchester?"

He regarded me intently. "You know I'm not supposed to tell you that."

"I know," I replied with defeat, swiveling back around to face the computer screen. "It's confidential."

I continued to read the rest of the obituary that ended with the statement that Alexander Fitzgerald was survived by a wife named Audrey and a three-year-old daughter named Wendy.

CHAPTER

Sixty-three

"Do you think I knew somehow?" I asked Jesse when I slipped into bed beside him that night. I reached for the hand lotion and rubbed some on my hands. "When I had that last flying dream, did I know my donor was named Alex? Had I read it or heard it somewhere? Maybe when I was on the operating table they mentioned his name and I heard it, stored it in my memory. That could explain this. But what about Ellen's blanket? Why would she name it Ouwix? Is she having flying dreams, too? Does she associate Alex with sleep and her blanket?"

Jesse closed the book he was reading and set it on the table. "I don't know. But whatever she's experiencing can't have anything to do with cellular memory because she was delivered before you got your new heart."

I pondered that. "You're right. Then could it be his ghost? They say children can sometimes see spirits better than we can. Maybe Alex is checking in on both of us." I sighed heavily. "Or maybe I'm losing my marbles. Maybe I heard the nurses mention his name in the OR, remembered it subconsciously, and now I talk in my sleep and she hears me say his name. We did share a room for the first year of her life."

"Who knows?" Jesse replied. "I never used to believe in the paranormal or magic, but lately I feel as if I'm seeing things for the first time."

"How so?"

He thought about it for a moment. "I'm still amazed by the fact that I was the one to deliver your heart to you. Then your sister contacted me out of the blue and now here we are—married. How could that all be a coincidence? And now I'm speaking to my brother again after ten years, and I have a feeling that if he and I can smooth things over, anything's possible and there might be hope with my parents, too. Ellen has named her blanket Ouwix, and you somehow knew that Alex Fitzgerald was your donor..."

"I thought that was supposed to be confidential," I said, raising an eyebrow.

"You figured that one out on your own," he reminded me.

I slid deeper beneath the covers and rested my cheek on his shoulder. He rubbed his thumb back and forth across my arm.

"Was I really just dreaming about flying?" I asked. "I know I've never actually gone flying at night. People can't fly. We don't have wings. But what does it mean? Is it astral projection? Or is it my spirit—somehow merged with Alexander's because I have his heart inside me now? And was my spirit merged with yours as well, because I had dreams about you, too? Or is it just my imagination making all this up?"

I thought about the book I'd read by Sophie Duncan—the author I met at the book signing who'd had an out-of-body experience when she crashed her car into a frozen lake. While she was unconscious, she'd learned things about her family she never could have known otherwise. Later she'd also found an old manuscript in her stepfather's attic that turned out to be written by her real father—a man she never knew existed before that.

My own situation was curiously similar…because even if I'd heard my donor's name on the operating table, it still didn't explain how I could know what he looked like.

Were our spirits somehow connected? Or was this just some sort of psychic ability?

Jesse turned out the light and held me close as he drifted off. I had a harder time falling asleep, however, because all I could think about was the life my donor had lived, and all he'd left behind. Since seeing his face in my dream, he was so much more real to me now.

Chapter Sixty-four

"We're almost there," I said, glancing back at Ellen in the rearview mirror. "Then we'll go to the playground and have a picnic."

I smiled at her and continued driving through the city of Manchester. I was looking for the fire station. I had done some online research about Alexander Fitzgerald and couldn't help myself. I was curious. I wanted to see where he'd lived and worked.

I would leave it at that, of course, because I'd already tried to contact his family and they'd made no overtures to meet me. I simply needed to see something of his life. That was all. Then I would go home and put it to rest.

Ellen looked out the window when I pulled over on Merrimack Street.

"Look at the fire station," I said. "See all the red trucks?"

She made no comment. She was more interested in flipping her fabric doll around like a gymnast, so I decided to move on. I checked my mirrors and pulled out onto the street again.

A few minutes later I turned onto Notre Dame and drove slowly, searching for Alexander's house. I spotted the right number and pulled over at the curb.

It was a large white three-story building that looked as if it had been converted into apartments. I wasn't sure what level he lived on, but it didn't matter. It was enough just to see his neighborhood and know he had walked along these sidewalks.

I'd done my homework and knew there was a playground across the street, so I turned off the car, got out and slung the lunch bag and diaper bag over my shoulder.

"Ready to go play?" I asked as I opened the back door and freed Ellen from the safety seat.

I carried her across the street and set her down in the play area where she toddled to the red slide.

Keeping my eye on her, I pulled the blanket out of the diaper bag and spread it out on the grass, then went to help her climb the steps of the play structure. She slid down the baby slide and shouted, "Again!" as she ran back around to the steps.

We were the only people in the park, but we enjoyed ourselves nonetheless. It was a beautiful day and I was grateful—as always—to be alive.

After awhile we sat down on the blanket and I opened the lunch bag. Ellen enjoyed some Cheerios and a juice box while I sat back and crossed my legs at the ankles, watching her chew.

Every so often I glanced across at the big white house on the other side of the street and thought about how the man who once lived there had died before his time. He was gone now. Gone from this world. But how generous of him to choose organ donation while he was still alive. I might not be sitting here today if he hadn't signed those papers. And where would Ellen be? Not with me. She would be somewhere else. With Diana most likely. Perhaps with Rick if things had been different.

The front door of the house opened just then. I sat up on my heels when a woman walked out with a small child. She locked the door behind her.

Good Lord. Was it Alexander's wife, Audrey? Her child looked to be about two or three years old. A girl.

My heart began to race and I wasn't sure what to do as they crossed the street and started walking toward us. *Does she know who I am?* Did she somehow sense her husband's heart beating in the playground across the street? Is that why she was walking toward us?

I managed to relax when she didn't make eye contact. She merely jogged to the play structure with her daughter who climbed the yellow bars and slid down the big, swirly slide.

Ellen turned and saw that another child had arrived, so she dropped her juice box and toddled back to the structure. I had no choice but to follow. Soon I was smiling pleasantly at the mother.

"Hi," she said. "Great day isn't it?"

"Gorgeous," I replied.

"Your daughter's adorable," she said. "How old?"

"Thirteen months," I replied. "How old is yours?"

"Wendy turned three a couple of weeks ago."

I swallowed hard. "Your daughter's name is Wendy?" I asked. "What a great name."

"Thank you. I loved Peter Pan when I was a kid. I always wanted to have a daughter and name her Wendy. Do you live near here?"

"No," I replied. "We live in Waltham. We're just passing through."

By now Ellen was trying to keep up with the climbing skills of Audrey's daughter, but she needed some help so I followed her to the big slide.

"Do you want to go down this one?" I asked. She hugged my leg. "Come on, we'll do it together." I sat down at the top. "Sit here on my lap."

Ellen climbed onto my lap and we slid down the twisty red slide. She laughed and said, "Again!" when we reached the bottom.

I took her hand and together we circled around the structure and climbed back up the steps.

"I confess," Audrey said when I returned to stand beside her, "that we only came out here because we saw the two of you from our front window. There aren't many kids on this street—at least none that are Wendy's age. She's an only child."

"My Ellen's an only, too," I told her.

"Oh. Are you married?" she asked.

I nodded. "Just recently, but my husband's working today." I paused. "You?"

She looked down and kicked the grass with the toe of her sneaker. "I was, but my husband passed away about a year ago. He was a firefighter. Died on the job."

I shifted uneasily. "I'm sorry to hear that."

She nodded. "Thank you. It's been a rough year but we're doing okay. Each day gets easier. It just makes me sad to think that Wendy won't remember her dad at all. She was so young when he died."

I watched the girls try to climb up the baby slide. "You'd be surprised what they remember. Even if it's just a subconscious memory."

"I hope so," she replied, "because he was a really good man. He had a good heart, you know?"

I swallowed over a lump in my throat. "I'm sure he did."

A strong breeze blew across the treetops and whispered through the leaves.

"Does Wendy like peach yogurt?" I asked. "I have a few tubs in my lunch bag and some juice boxes. Would you like to join us?"

"That sounds lovely," she replied. "Wendy! Want a snack?"

The two girls came running, and we all sat down on the blanket to enjoy ourselves in the sun.

Epilogue

On the day I met Audrey Fitzgerald, I understood that coincidences like this make our world a remarkable place to live in.

If that's all they are...*coincidences.*

Personally, I believe certain things are meant to be and "coincidence" is far too casual a word for what happens to many of us.

For a full hour, Ellen and I played in the park with Audrey and her daughter. Then we said our good-byes and I drove home to Waltham where Jesse was waiting for me with supper on the table.

I told him about my afternoon with the wife of my organ donor. When he asked if I told her who I was, I said no. I chose to respect her privacy, and it was unlikely I would ever see her again.

But oh, how lovely and kind she was. I resolved to say a daily prayer for her future happiness. I hoped and prayed that one day she would rediscover joy—as I had discovered it upon the blessing of a second chance at life, thanks to her husband.

I came a long way. I faced death and fought my way back to a level of health where I will never cease to appreciate the miracles of life and the goodness of humanity around me.

What a gift we are given each day when we rise. The world is beautiful, and isn't it wonderful to think that dreams can take us to the most incredible places?

Never stop believing that. Always look to the future. And keep dreaming.

Questions for Discussion

1. How do the actions of Jesse and Rick reveal their true characters in the first twenty-one chapters of the novel?
2. Though Rick is a villain in Jesse's eyes, is there any sign of goodness in Rick? If so, where? Do you believe he is portrayed fairly in this novel? If you read the previous book, *The Color of Hope*, what are your thoughts about Rick? Is he really as bad as some of these characters make him out to be?
3. Nadia's section begins with a reference to her recurring dream of flying. Have you ever dreamed you were flying? Do you believe in astral projection?
4. Is there another recurring dream you have that has some meaning in your life? If so, what is it?
5. Why do you think Jesse was attracted to Nadia at first sight, and not Diana, given they are identical twins?
6. Jesse couldn't help Angela and that part of his past haunts him. How do you feel this plays into his actions and decisions throughout the rest of the novel? Do you believe he lets go of this guilt in the end?
7. Nadia falls for Jesse quickly. Do you feel she was desperate to have a loving partner and father for her child? Or was she truly meant to be with Jesse?
8. Toward the end of the novel, Nadia is still asking questions about the meaning of her dreams. She remains skeptical. Do you believe there is an answer to her experience? If so, what do you believe it is?

9. When Nadia meets Audrey in the playground, should she have told her who she was? How do you think Audrey would have reacted?
10. The word “dream” has many meanings. What connotations are present in this novel?

For more information about this book and others in the Color of Heaven series, please visit the author's website at www.juliannemaclean.com. While you're there, be sure to sign up for Julianne's newsletter to stay informed about upcoming releases as they are announced.

Read on for an excerpt from

The COLOR *of a* MEMORY

book five in the Color of Heaven series.

Prologue

Audrey Fitzgerald

I didn't know it at the time, but it was something quite extraordinary that drew my daughter Wendy to the window that morning. In my ignorance, I was simply pleased to have an excuse to leave the dirty dishes behind for later when she said, "Look, Mommy." Her tiny nose was pressed to the glass. "A little girl..."

Wendy was three years old. It was just the two of us then, living alone together in a ground-floor apartment in Manchester, Connecticut. Wendy had very little memory of her father who had died the year before.

He was a firefighter and a great hero on many levels, though I didn't always believe that. We'd had our ups and downs, Alex and I.

But on that particular day, all that mattered to me was my daughter's happiness. As a result, when she asked to go outside and play with the little girl enjoying a picnic with her mother across the street, I was quick to grab our jackets and go.

"Do you live near here?" I asked the girl's mother as we stood in the playground watching our daughters run around in circles.

"We live in Waltham," she replied in a friendly tone of voice. "We're just passing through." Then she noticed her daughter, who looked to be about eighteen months old, struggling to climb up the steps to the big swirly slide. "Pardon me for a second," she said.

She went to help her, and down they went, laughing and squealing.

It was a moment I appreciated because it had been a somber year since my husband's death.

Oh, how I missed that feeling…being able to laugh and experience such joy over simply being alive.

"I confess," I said to the woman when she returned to stand beside me, "that we only came out here because we saw the two of you from our front window. There aren't many kids on this street—at least none Wendy's age. She's an only child."

"My Ellen's an only, too," she told me.

"Are you married?" I asked, not knowing why I suddenly blurted out such a personal question, but I was curious for some reason. There was something familiar about this woman.

She nodded, but didn't meet my gaze. "Just recently, but my husband's working today. You?"

I looked down at my running shoes and wondered when I would be able to answer that question without feeling like I wanted to crawl into bed, curl up in a ball and draw the covers up to my ears.

"I was," I replied, "but my husband passed away about a year ago. He was a firefighter. Died on the job."

The woman said nothing for a moment, then she, too, looked down at the grass and ran the toe of her shoe over a brown patch. "I'm sorry to hear that."

Funny, how the mention of death always casts such a dark shadow over any conversation. I wished I hadn't said anything. I really had to learn to keep my tragic widowhood to myself. Why couldn't I just smile and give the subject of marriage a wide berth?

Later, the woman invited Wendy and me to join her on the blanket for some yogurt and juice. Soon we were chatting about preschools and kid-friendly menu options, and for reasons I didn't understand at the time, she began asking questions about Alex.

Given the circumstances of my relationship with my late husband and how we came to be together, I should have been more suspicious of her—because when it came to Alex and other women, I'd been burned before. Quite literally, in fact.

But this stranger in the park had a way of making me let down my guard. Before I knew it, I was spilling out my whole life story to her—to this person I would later learn was connected to me in the most profound way, in a way I never could have imagined. At least not at the time.

But isn't that what life's all about? Learning new things about ourselves and making sense of our destinies?

How extraordinary it is when all the puzzle pieces finally come together and we are able to see the whole picture…and behold something beautiful.

Chapter One

If someone told me years ago that one day I would become "the other woman," I wouldn't have believed it. I'd been raised by two happily married parents with an iron-clad set of rules about family values.

"You don't cheat," my father said to all of us on a regular basis, pointing his chubby finger at the air. "It's a simple matter of honor."

He and my mother could have been the poster children for every self-help book on the market about how to succeed at marriage. After thirty years, they still held hands and flirted with each other as if they'd just spoken their wedding vows the day before.

I'd always imagined I would end up in a relationship just like theirs—because didn't people say girls usually married carbon copies of their fathers?

I suppose I blew that rule out of the water on the day I met Alex Fitzgerald for the first time—because he was exactly the sort of man my father always warned me *against.*

Too handsome for his own good. And Lord, did he know it.

Chapter Two

"Are you Alex Fitzgerald?" I asked as I pulled back the blue curtain in the ER and regarded the dark-haired firefighter on the bed. He wore a black T-shirt and faded blue jeans, and smirked at me like he was Colin Farrell.

"Yep."

Standing with my pen hovering over the chart on my clipboard, I said, "Can you tell me what happened?"

There was a second firefighter in the room as well. He stood beside the bed. Tall and broad-shouldered, he was equally handsome but with honey-colored hair. He bowed his head and chuckled.

Alex gave him a smack with the back of his hand before he answered my question. "Don't make fun, David, or my pretty nurse will ask you to leave."

My eyes lifted and I regarded them both without humor.

"He dropped a fire extinguisher on his foot," David explained.

My next enquiry was directed at the patient. "What part of your foot, exactly?"

David chuckled again.

"What did I just tell ya?" Alex said to his friend with a laugh. Then he swept me a flirtatious glance with those dark-lashed brown eyes, and smiled. "Though maybe it would be *better* if he left. Is he distracting you, Nurse…?" He sat forward to squint at my badge. "Nurse Audrey. That's a very pretty name."

I lowered the clipboard to my side and glanced from one firefighter to the other. They each wore tight T-shirts that shamelessly flaunted their muscular upper bodies. The testosterone in the room was palpable, but I'd had a rough morning with a difficult pediatric case—possible leukemia—that left me in no mood for barroom pickup lines.

"Any smoke inhalation?" I asked, pushing my glasses up the bridge of my nose.

David, the blonde one, was quick to pipe in and answer the question. "No, you've got it all wrong. Alex was stuffing his face with French fries at the station and his hands were all greasy. He picked up an empty extinguisher to move it off a chair so he could sit down and take a load off, but it slipped through his fingers. Ketchup flew everywhere, and it was quite the ordeal. He thinks something's broken."

I inclined my head at Alex, who didn't appear to be in much pain at all. "Is that what happened?"

"It's dangerous work sometimes," he replied.

I glanced down at Alex's sneaker. "Well, hotshot. You're going to have to remove that shoe so the doctor can examine you. The sock, too."

Without warning, one of the other nurses whipped the privacy curtain back and I jumped. "Can you come over to bed six?" she asked. "I need help with an IV."

"I'll be right there," I smoothly replied. Then I met my patient's gaze. "I'll be back in two minutes."

"I'll be waiting," he replied with a playful note of seduction in his voice that made me shake my head in disbelief as I turned away.

~

When I pulled back the curtain on Mr. Hotshot Firefighter a few minutes later, he was sitting up on the edge of the bed.

Shirtless.

Though I was a practical and levelheaded woman by nature, I couldn't ignore the fact that I was standing before a ridiculously extravagant plethora of bronzed, rippling muscles that must have taken years of workouts at the gym to achieve. I couldn't help but laugh at the proud spectacle before me. This man was unbelievable. "I said the shoe, not the shirt."

"No, I'm sure you said the shirt," he innocently replied. "Don't you have to listen to my heart or something? Take my blood pressure…I did feel a bit woozy when it happened."

It had been an utterly wretched day for the most part, so I decided at last to surrender to the comedy of this moment. Striding forward, I removed my stethoscope from the pocket of my uniform and kept my eyes fixed on his as I touched the scope to his chest. "Where did your friend go?"

"I told him I didn't need a babysitter," Alex replied. "He's probably chatting up some young nursing student by now."

I nodded my head. "I see. You two are quite the pair. I can't imagine what sort of trouble you must get into on a Saturday night."

"Oh, no," Alex replied. "We're not like that."

I chuckled. "Says the man who couldn't wait to strip off his T-shirt for the poor unsuspecting nurse."

He slanted me a look. "Poor, unsuspecting? Pardon me for sayin' so, Nurse Audrey, but those aren't the words I would use to describe *you*."

With no intention of falling for his charms, I gave no reply and focused on the task of taking his blood pressure.

"I guess I don't need to ask you to roll up your sleeve… since you aren't wearing one," I mentioned with dry sarcasm as I wrapped the cuff around his generous bicep.

"Do you have a boyfriend, Nurse Audrey?" Alex asked as I pumped air into the BP cuff.

Timing the pulse in the crook of his arm, I chose to ignore the question. Then I tugged at the Velcro and removed the cuff. "Blood pressure looks good," I said. "You're healthy as a horse."

The resident doctor walked in. "Hey there," he casually said, sliding his hands into the pockets of his lab coat. "What's up?"

"This is Alex Fitzgerald," I explained. "He's a firefighter and he dropped an extinguisher on his foot. He thinks it might be broken."

"Sounds like you had an off day." Dr. Grant moved around the foot of the bed and patted the mattress. "How about swinging your legs right up here."

Backing out of the way, I watched while Dr. Grant examined Alex's foot. He pressed the pads of his thumbs in different areas and asked all sorts of questions.

He made no comment about the fact that Alex was shirtless.

"It does look like something might be broken," Dr. Grant said to me. "We're going to need an X-ray to see what we're dealing with, so take him up to radiology and let me know as soon as you have the results."

"Sure," I replied.

After he left, Alex inclined his head at me and spoke cheerfully. "Looks like we'll get to spend some more time together, Nurse Audrey."

"Not until you put your shirt back on," I replied matter-of-factly as I went to fetch a wheelchair.

Over the next five hours, I kept abreast of Alex's case. The X-ray images revealed that he had broken two of his metatarsals, which are good-sized bones in his foot. This surprised me because most people are pasty gray and do a fair bit of moaning and complaining when they arrive in the ER with even the smallest fracture.

But Alex was a trooper and managed to get through all the poking and prodding with a sense of humor, pouring on the charm to all the nurses, even the older ones. Especially them. After a while I began to relax and stopped assuming he was just trying to pick me up. In fact, it lifted my spirits to see the older ladies blush.

When at last he was discharged with a cast boot on his foot, I was just finishing my shift, so I volunteered to push him in the wheelchair onto the elevator to take him down to the front lobby.

"You never answered my question," he said when the elevator doors closed and we were alone.

"What question was that?"

"I asked if you had a boyfriend," he reminded me.

For a long moment I stared at the floor indicator above the doors and watched the numbers count down. When the display flashed L and I knew it was time to get off, I said with a sigh of defeat, "No, I don't have a boyfriend."

The doors opened. I pushed the chair forward.

As we were rolling out, he tipped his head all the way back to look up at me, and I found myself smiling down at his face, which was no less handsome from that angle.

"You're a good nurse," he said. "I'm glad it was you today."

"I'll bet you say that to all the girls," I replied with a smile.

"Nope, just you. So how about you let me buy you dinner?"

"I don't think so."

"At least tell me your last name. Or give me your phone number."

I grinned down at him. "Not a chance." Then I briefly glanced up to make sure I wasn't about to steer him down a steep flight of stairs. That wouldn't be good.

He faced forward as well. "Then don't be surprised if you see me again next week with some other random ailment. Maybe I'll develop a pain in my side that will take hours to diagnose."

"Didn't you ever hear the story about the boy who cried wolf?" I asked. "That didn't end well."

He tilted his head back again. "Then maybe you should just give me your number."

I laughed and shook my head at him then realized we were about to collide with a woman who was standing directly in our path to the door.

I pulled the chair to a halt and Alex jolted forward.

"Melanie," he said, seeming startled to see her.

"Hey." She glanced at me suspiciously, then adjusted her purse strap on her shoulder. "Who's this?"

"This is Audrey," Alex replied. "She's my nurse. Audrey, this is Melanie."

"Hi," I casually said, waving a hand.

Melanie was tall and supermodel-skinny with blonde hair, full lips and big eyes—eyes that glared at me with venom.

"I thought David was picking me up," Alex said to her.

"I told him I'd do it," she replied. "Why didn't you call me earlier? I would have come right away. Is it broken?"

He lifted the cast boot to show her. "Yeah. Guess I'll be off work for a few weeks."

"Bummer," Melanie said. "Are you ready to go? I can bring the car around."

"That would be great. Thanks."

Melanie hurried off, leaving Alex and me alone to wait inside. I set the brake on the chair and sat down on the window ledge to face him.

"Who's Melanie?" I asked point blank. "Your sister? Cousin? Housekeeper, maybe?"

His eyes were fixed on the view of the parking lot outside the glass. "She's not my girlfriend," he said. "Well, she sort of is. She *was*."

I held up a hand. "Don't bother to explain. It's none of my business."

We waited in silence for a moment.

"So I guess dinner Friday night is out of the question?" he asked, turning his head to look at me.

"Yep. Totally out of the question."

His chest rose and fell with a heavy sigh, and he nodded his head, as if he wasn't surprised.

Melanie came speeding up to the entrance in a sporty little lime-green Volkswagen convertible. She pulled to a halt and got out to open the passenger side door.

I rolled Alex outside, set the brake again, and he hobbled out of the chair and into the front seat.

"Thanks, Audrey," he said as I backed up and rolled the chair out of the way.

"No problem. Take care, now."

He shut the car door and Melanie hit the gas. They sped off into the hazy evening sunset. For a moment I stood alone, watching the car grow distant, then I returned inside to grab my stuff and go home.

Over the next few days, I thought about Alex Fitzgerald more often than I cared to admit and it bothered me how much he was on my mind. I hardly knew the guy, and he certainly wasn't my type because he was too much of a flirt. I had seen dozens of patients that day. Why should I be thinking of *him*?

Because he looked great shirtless?

Needless to say, I made sure I worked hard to purge him from my mind, but I also felt sorry for Melanie who was clearly devoted to him while he was asking other women out on dates.

I decided I wouldn't want to be in her shoes. Not in a million years.

Looking back on it, I wish I had mentioned the encounter to someone, because that's when the phone calls began. It would have been helpful to have had a record of everything.

Chapter Three

The first call occurred when I arrived home from the movies on a Saturday night. The call display said "Private Caller," so I picked it up. "Hello?"

My greeting was met with a few seconds of silence, which made me think it was a telemarketer. I was about to press the end call button, but the unknown caller hung up before I had a chance to.

It happened again the following morning at eight o'clock, waking me from a very deep sleep. I flopped across the bed and answered groggily, "Hello?"

Again I was met with silence on the other end, then *click*. The line went dead.

"Thanks a lot," I replied as I ended the call and tried, unsuccessfully, to go back to sleep.

How foolish I was to think it was a wrong number, but my night shift hours that week had left me in a daze.

But eventually, I *would* wake from it.

I didn't work another shift until Tuesday night, which gave me time to attend a spinning class that morning and meet my friend Cathy for lunch downtown.

Cathy and I had known each other since high school and I was her maid of honor the previous summer when she married Bob, the guy she met in college.

Bob was an electrician but he was working with some filmmaker pals on a reality TV show about rewiring old houses. Bob was smart and funny and we all knew he'd make a terrific host. They just had to pitch their idea to a network willing to take a chance on the idea.

As for Cathy, she was the most generous, easygoing person I knew, and she worked part-time for an insurance company.

"Audrey, why don't we go down to the fire station after lunch and ask how that hot firefighter's doing?" she suggested when our soups and salads arrived. "I'm sure someone will know. Didn't you say he brought a friend to the ER? We could ask that guy."

"I'm not going down there," I replied, "because I have no desire to find out how he's doing. And why do you keep bringing it up?"

"Because you told me what he looked like shirtless and what a jerk he was for cheating on his girlfriend. You *never* talk about patients like that. Isn't there some rule about confidentiality?"

"I also never went out with him," I replied, "so in actuality, he didn't cheat on his girlfriend. And confidentiality hasn't been breached because I didn't tell you his name."

She wagged her salad fork at me. "But he would have cheated on her if you had said yes to the date."

I shook my head. "I still don't even know if she *was* his girlfriend. He was pretty vague about it."

"There, you see?" Cathy said. "You're still curious about him."

I looked down at my minestrone soup. "No, I'm not."

"You're the biggest liar I know."

"Maybe so," I replied with a chuckle, "but I'm still not going down to the fire station."

I had been manning the nurse's station for a few hours that night when Jason, the clerk beside me, tapped me on the shoulder. "Audrey?"

I looked up from the computer screen to find myself staring blankly at Alex Fitzgerald. He stood on crutches on the other side of the desk.

"Hey," I said, blinking my eyes to try and gain some focus. "What are you doing here? Is everything okay?"

As if he were pulling a rabbit out of a hat, he whipped out a big bunch of colorful spring flowers and held them out. "These are for you."

Leaning back in my chair, folding my arms across my chest, I laughed. "What for?"

"To say thank you."

I regarded him skeptically. "I was just doing my job."

"But you did it brilliantly." He glanced at Jason who was standing beside me, listening to our conversation with interest. "I'm here to ask her out for dinner, but I'm afraid she's going to say no."

Jason nudged me with his elbow. *Hard*. "Come on, Audrey. Throw the guy a bone. He came all the way down here on crutches. The least you could do is have something to eat with him."

"I'm working," I reminded them both.

"You have a supper break coming up," Jason was happy to add. "She usually eats in the cafeteria," he told Alex.

Alex held out the flowers again. "Perfect. I love cafeteria food, and these need to be put in water."

Jason reached across the desk to take them. "I'll handle that."

"You're not helping," I called out to Jason over my shoulder as he went off in search of a suitable container.

Alex smiled at me.

"How's your foot?" I asked him.

"Better," he replied. "I'm getting around okay. How's everything with you?"

"Fine and dandy."

We regarded each other for a long, intense moment, then I laughed softly in defeat.

"So is that a yes?" Alex asked, tilting his head to the side.

Jason returned with the flowers, set them down on the desk in front of me and nudged me again with his elbow.

I let out a breathless sigh. "I guess so. As long as you promise to keep your shirt on this time."

Alex held up a few fingers. "Scout's honor. At least for today."

I tossed my pencil onto the desk and went to grab my purse, feeling quite certain that agreeing to have dinner with Alex Fitzgerald was going to be one of the worst mistakes of my life.

Other Books in the Color of Heaven Series

The COLOR *of* HEAVEN

A deeply emotional tale about Sophie Duncan, a successful columnist whose world falls apart after her daughter's unexpected illness and her husband's shocking affair. When it seems nothing else could possibly go wrong, her car skids off an icy road and plunges into a frozen lake. There, in the cold dark depths of the water, a profound and extraordinary experience unlocks the surprising secrets from Sophie's past, and teaches her what it means to truly live...and love.

Full of surprising twists and turns and a near-death experience that will leave you breathless, this story is not to be missed.

"A gripping, emotional tale you'll want to read in one sitting."
– *New York Times* bestselling author, Julia London

"Brilliantly poignant mainstream tale."
– 4 ½ starred review, *Romantic Times*

The COLOR *of* DESTINY

Eighteen years ago a teenage pregnancy changed Kate Worthington's life forever. Faced with many difficult decisions, she chose to follow her heart and embrace an uncertain future with the father of her baby – her devoted first love.

At the same time, in another part of the world, sixteen-year-old Ryan Hamilton makes his own share of mistakes, but learns important lessons along the way. Twenty years later, Kate's and Ryan's paths cross in a way they could never expect, which makes them question the possibility of destiny. Even when all seems hopeless, could it be that everything happens for a reason, and we end up exactly where we are meant to be?

The COLOR *of* HOPE

Diana Moore has led a charmed life. She is the daughter of a wealthy senator and lives a glamorous city life, confident that her handsome live-in boyfriend Rick is about to propose. But everything is turned upside down when she learns of a mysterious woman who works nearby – a woman who is her identical mirror image.

Diana is compelled to discover the truth about this woman's identity, but the truth leads her down a path of secrets, betrayals, and shocking discoveries about her past. These discoveries follow her like a shadow.

Then she meets Dr. Jacob Peterson—a brilliant cardiac surgeon with an uncanny ability to heal those who are broken. With his help, Diana embarks upon a journey to restore her belief in the human spirit, and recover a sense of hope - that happiness, and love, may still be within reach for those willing to believe in second chances.

The COLOR *of* A DREAM

Nadia Carmichael has had a lifelong run of bad luck. It begins on the day she is born, when she is separated from her identical twin sister and put up for adoption. Twenty-seven years later, not long after she is finally reunited with her twin and is expecting her first child, Nadia falls victim to a mysterious virus and requires a heart transplant.

Now recovering from the surgery with a new heart, Nadia is haunted by a recurring dream that sets her on a path to discover the identity of her donor. Her efforts are thwarted, however, when the father of her baby returns to sue for custody of their child. It's not until Nadia learns of his estranged brother Jesse that she begins to explore the true nature of her dreams, and discover what her new heart truly needs and desires...

The COLOR *of* A MEMORY

Audrey Fitzgerald believed she was married to the perfect man - a heroic firefighter who saved lives, even beyond his own death. But a year later she meets a mysterious woman who has some unexplained connection to her husband....

Soon Audrey discovers that her husband was keeping secrets and she is compelled to dig into his past. Little does she know... this journey of self-discovery will lead her down a path to a new and different future - a future she never could have imagined.

The COLOR *of* LOVE

Carla Matthews is a single mother struggling to make ends meet and give her daughter Kaleigh a decent upbringing. When Kaleigh's absent father Seth—a famous alpine climber who never wanted to be tied down—begs for a second chance at fatherhood, Carla is hesitant because she doesn't want to pin her hopes on a man who is always seeking another mountain to scale. A man who was never willing to stay put in one place and raise a family.

But when Seth's plane goes missing after a crash landing in the harsh Canadian wilderness, Carla must wait for news...Is he dead or alive? Will the wreckage ever be found?

One year later, after having given up all hope, Carla receives a phone call that shocks her to her core. A man has been found, half-dead, floating on an iceberg in the North Atlantic, uttering her name. Is this Seth? And is it possible that he will come home to her and Kaleigh at last, and be the man she always dreamed he would be?

The COLOR *of* THE SEASON

Boston cop, Josh Wallace, is having the worst day of his life. First, he's dumped by the woman he was about to propose to, then everything goes downhill from there when he is shot in the line of duty. While recovering in the hospital, he can't seem to forget the woman he wanted to marry, nor can he make sense of the vivid images that flashed before his eyes when he was wounded on the job. Soon, everything he once believed about his life begins to shift when he meets Leah James, an enigmatic resident doctor who somehow holds the key to both his past and his future…

Praise for Julianne MacLean's Historical Romances

"MacLean's compelling writing turns this simple, classic love story into a richly emotional romance, and by combining engaging characters with a unique, vividly detailed setting, she has created an exceptional tale for readers who hunger for something a bit different in their historical romances."

—*BOOKLIST*

"You can always count on Julianne MacLean to deliver ravishing romance that will keep you turning pages until the wee hours of the morning."

—Teresa Medeiros

"Julianne MacLean's writing is smart, thrilling, and sizzles with sensuality."

—Elizabeth Hoyt

"Scottish romance at its finest, with characters to cheer for, a lush love story, and rousing adventure. I was captivated from the very first page. When it comes to exciting Highland romance, Julianne MacLean delivers."

—Laura Lee Guhrke

"She is just an all-around wonderful writer, and I look forward to reading everything she writes."

—*Romance Junkies*

About the Author

Julianne MacLean is a USA Today bestselling author of many historical romances, including The Highlander Series with St. Martin's Press and her popular American Heiress Series with Avon/Harper Collins. She also writes contemporary mainstream fiction, and The Color of Heaven was a USA Today bestseller. She is a three-time RITA finalist, and has won numerous awards, including the Booksellers' Best Award, the Book Buyer's Best Award, and a Reviewers' Choice Award from Romantic Times for Best Regency Historical of 2005. She lives in Nova Scotia with her husband and daughter, and is a dedicated member of Romance Writers of Atlantic Canada. Please visit Julianne's website for more information and to subscribe to her mailing list to stay informed about upcoming releases.

Other Books by Julianne MacLean

The American Heiress Series:

To Marry the Duke
An Affair Most Wicked
My Own Private Hero
Love According to Lily
Portrait of a Lover
Surrender to a Scoundrel

The Pembroke Palace Series:

In My Wildest Fantasies
The Mistress Diaries
When a Stranger Loves Me
Married By Midnight
A Kiss Before the Wedding - A Pembroke Palace Short Story
Seduced at Sunset

The Highlander Series:

Captured by the Highlander
Claimed by the Highlander
Seduced by the Highlander
The Rebel – A Highland Short Story

The Royal Trilogy:

Be My Prince
Princess in Love
The Prince's Bride

Harlequin Historical Romances:

Prairie Bride
The Marshal and Mrs. O'Malley
Adam's Promise

Time Travel Romance

Taken by the Cowboy

Contemporary Fiction:

The Color of Heaven
The Color of Destiny
The Color of Hope
The Color of a Dream
The Color of a Memory
The Color of Love
The Color of the Season
The Color of Joy

Made in the USA
Lexington, KY
19 October 2015